Tawny-Lynn leaned into Chaz, her body trembling. Ever since that awful accident, she'd felt alone.

She'd learned to deal with it and to stand on her own, but for just a moment, she allowed herself the comfort of Chaz's arms.

Tension slowly seeped from her tightly wound muscles. She felt the warmth of his arms encircling her, the soft rise and fall of his chest against her cheek, the whisper of his breath against her ear.

But the safety felt too wonderful for her to fantasize that it would last.

Finally she raised her gaze to his. His eyes darkened with concern and other emotions that made her want to reach up and touch his cheek.

Kiss his lips.

COLD CASE AT CAMDEN CROSSING

—

RITA HERRON

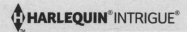

HARLEQUIN® INTRIGUE®

To Dana for her support and help on this book!

Recycling programs
for this product may
not exist in your area.

ISBN-13: 978-0-373-74784-9

COLD CASE AT CAMDEN CROSSING

Copyright © 2013 by Rita B. Herron

Printed in U.S.A.

ABOUT THE AUTHOR

Award-winning author Rita Herron wrote her first book when she was twelve, but didn't think real people grew up to be writers. Now she writes so she doesn't have to get a *real* job. A former kindergarten teacher and workshop leader, she traded storytelling to kids for writing romance, and now she writes romantic comedies and romantic suspense. She lives in Georgia with her own romance hero and three kids. She loves to hear from readers, so please write her at P.O. Box 921225, Norcross, GA 30092-1225, or visit her website, www.ritaherron.com.

Books by Rita Herron

HARLEQUIN INTRIGUE

*Nighthawk Island
††Guardian Angel Investigations
‡Guardian Angel Investigations:
   Lost and Found
**Bucking Bronc Lodge

CAST OF CHARACTERS

Sheriff Chaz Camden—He became a lawman to find out who kidnapped his sister and if she's still alive, but the secret to the cold case lies with Tawny-Lynn Boulder, a woman who claims she doesn't remember what happened the day his sister and hers went missing.

Tawny-Lynn Boulder—She's been tormented for years over her sister and Ruth Camden's disappearance, but someone doesn't want her to remember what happened that day....

Ruth Camden—She went missing after a terrible bus crash seven years ago. Is she dead or alive?

Peyton Boulder—Tawny-Lynn's sister also disappeared. Did someone kidnap her or did she run away?

Gerome Camden—He and his wife want justice for their daughter, and crucified Tawny-Lynn after the accident by accusing her of covering for a killer.

J J McMullen—When Peyton dumped him for another man, was he mad enough to kill her to get revenge?

Coach Jim Wake—He was devastated when half of his softball team died in the bus crash—did he know who Peyton was seeing?

Barry Dothan—This mentally challenged man is obsessed with taking pictures of the girls on the softball team. Did he do something to Ruth and Peyton?

Keith Plumbing—A handyman who did odd jobs in Camden Crossing and Sunset Mesa, a neighboring town where two teens have also gone missing. Is he responsible for the girls' disappearance?

Prologue

Sixteen-year-old Tawny-Lynn Boulder gripped the edge of the seat as something slammed into the back of the bus and sent it careening to the right, skimming the guardrail.

Tires squealed, the driver lost control and sparks spewed from the sides as they swerved back and forth. Screams from the other girls on the softball team echoed around her. Glass shattered.

She glanced sideways as she struggled to keep from pitching into the aisle. The ravine loomed only a few feet away.

Her body bounced against the seat as the bus rolled. Her sister, Peyton, cried out as her head hit the roof of the bus. Someone's shoe sailed over the seat. A gym bag clumped down the aisle.

Peyton's best friend, Ruth, clawed at her with bloody hands.

Then the bus was sliding, skidding, skating toward the edge of the ravine. Metal screeched and gears ground as they broke through the railing. For a terrifying second, the bus was suspended, teeter-ing on the edge of the cliff.

More screams and blood flying. Then the vehicle crashed over the edge of the embankment, plung-ing downward into the ravine below.

"Peyton!" Tawny-Lynn cried.

The force threw Peyton over the seat. More glass rained inside as the bus slammed into a boulder.

Her head hit something, her shoulder ramming into the opposite side of the bus. For a moment, she lost consciousness.

Seconds or maybe minutes later, she stirred, her body aching, her leg twisted beneath a gnarled metal seat edge. She searched for Peyton, terrified she was dead.

They'd had a fight earlier. Stupid sister stuff.

She wanted to make up.

Suddenly smoke began to fill the bus. She strug-gled to free her leg, but she was trapped.

Someone was crying in the back. But the other screams had subsided.

She managed to raise herself and look into the aisle.

God, no… One of the girls wasn't moving.

And Peyton and Ruth, where were they?

The bus rocked back and forth as if hanging on to a boulder. The smoke grew thicker. Somewhere through the gray haze, she saw flames shooting up toward the night sky.

She coughed and choked, then everything went dark.

Chapter One

"Your daddy is dead."

Tawny-Lynn gripped the phone with sweaty palms, then sank onto the bench in her garden. The roses that she'd groomed and loved so much suddenly smelled sickly sweet.

"Did you hear me, Tawny-Lynn?"

She nodded numbly, fighting the bitter memories assaulting her, then realized her father's lawyer Bentley Bannister couldn't see her, so she muttered a quiet yes.

But the memories crashed back. The bus accident. The fire. The screams. Then half the team was dead.

Somehow she'd survived, although she had no idea how. She'd lost time when she'd blacked out. Couldn't remember what had happened after the fire broke out.

But when she'd woken up, her sister and her friend Ruth were gone.

She'd been terrified they were dead. But the police had never found their bodies.

They had escaped somehow. Although half of Camden Crossing thought they'd fallen to foul play, that the accident hadn't been an accident. That a predator had caused the crash, then abducted Peyton and Ruth.

Just like a predator had taken two girls a year before that from a neighboring town.

Bannister cleared his throat, his voice gruff. "He was sick for a while, but I guess you knew that already."

No, she didn't. But then again, she wasn't surprised. His drinking and the two-pack-a-day cigarette habit had to have caught up with him at some point.

"Anyway, I suppose you'll want to be here to oversee the memorial service."

"No, go ahead with that," Tawny-Lynn said. Her father wouldn't have wanted her to come.

Wouldn't have wanted her near him.

Like everyone else in town, he'd blamed her. If she'd remembered more, seen what had happened, they might have been able to find Peyton and Ruth.

"Are you sure? He was your father, Tawny-Lynn."

"My father hated me after Peyton went missing," Tawny-Lynn said bluntly.

"Sugar, he was upset—"

"Don't defend him," she said. "I left Camden

Crossing and him behind years ago." Although the crash and screams had followed her, still haunted her in her dreams.

A tense heartbeat passed. "All right. But the ranch... Well, White Forks is yours now."

The ranch. God... She bowed her head and inhaled deep breaths. The familiar panic attack was threatening. She had to ward it off.

"You will come back and take care of the ranch, won't you?"

Take care of it as in *live* there? No way.

She massaged her temple, a migraine threatening. Just the thought of returning to the town that hated her made her feel ill.

"Tawny-Lynn?"

"Just hang a for-sale sign in the yard."

His breath wheezed out, reminding her that he was a heavy smoker, too. "About the ranch. Your father let it go the last few years. I don't think you'll get anything for it unless you do some upkeep."

Tawny-Lynn glanced around her small, cozy apartment. It was nestled in Austin, a city big enough to support businesses. A city where no one knew her and where she could get lost in the crowd.

Where no one hated her for the past.

The last thing she wanted to do was have to revisit the house where her life had fallen apart.

But her conversation with her accountant about her new landscape business echoed in her head, and she realized that selling the property could provide the money she needed to make her business a success.

She had to go back and clean up the ranch, then sell it.

Then she'd finally be done with Camden Crossing and the people in it for good.

SHERIFF CHAZ CAMDEN glanced at the missing-persons report that had just come in over the fax. Another young girl, barely eighteen.

Gone.

Vanished from a town in New Mexico in the middle of the night. A runaway or a kidnapping?

He studied the picture, his gut knotting. She was a brunette like his sister, Ruth, had been. Same innocent smile. Her life ahead of her.

And according to her parents, a happy well-adjusted teenager who planned to attend college. A girl who never came home after her curfew.

They thought someone had kidnapped her just as he'd suspected someone had abducted Ruth and Peyton after that horrendous bus crash.

Not that New Mexico was close enough to Camden Crossing, Texas, that he thought it was the same sicko.

But close enough to remind him of the tragedy that had torn his family apart.

The door to the sheriff's office burst open, and he frowned as his father walked in. Gerome Camden, a banker and astute businessman, owned half the town and had raised him with an iron fist. The two of them had tangled when he was growing up, but Ruth had been his father's pet, and it had nearly killed him when she'd disappeared.

"We need to talk," his dad said without preamble.

Chaz shoved the flier about the missing girl beneath a stack of folders, knowing it would trigger one of his father's tirades. Although judging from the scowl on his aging face, he was already upset about something.

Chaz leaned back in his chair. "What is it, Dad?"

"Tawny-Lynn Boulder is back in town."

Chaz stifled a reaction. "Really? I heard she didn't want a memorial service for her father."

The gray streaks in his father's hair glinted in the sunlight streaming through the window. "Who could blame her? Eugene Boulder was a common drunk."

"Guess that's how he dealt with Peyton going missing."

Unlike his father who'd just turned plain mean. Although he'd heard Boulder *had* been a mean drunk.

"Don't make excuses for that bastard. If Tawny-Lynn hadn't faked that amnesia, we might have found Ruth a long time ago."

Chaz started to point out for the hundredth time that the doctors said the amnesia was real, but his father didn't give him time.

"Bannister handled the will. The ranch is hers."

Chaz sighed and tapped his foot under the desk. "That's no surprise. Tawny-Lynn was his only living relative. It makes sense he'd leave her White Forks."

His father's cheeks reddened as he leaned forward on the desk, his anger gaining steam. "You need to make sure she doesn't stay. This town barely survived that girl years ago. We don't need her here as a reminder of the worst thing that ever happened in Camden Crossing."

Chaz had heard enough. He stood slowly, determined to control the anger building inside him. Just because his father was a big shot in Camden Crossing, he refused to let him push him around.

"Dad, I'm the sheriff, not your personal peon." His father opened his mouth, his hands balling into fists, but Chaz motioned him to hear him out. "My job is to protect the citizens of this town."

"That's what I'm saying—"

"No, it's not. You all ran roughshod over a sixteen-year-old girl who was traumatized and confused. And now you want me to make her leave town?" He slammed his own fist on the desk. "For God's sake, Tawny-Lynn lost her sister that day. She was suffering, too."

She'd been injured, although someone had pulled her free from the fire just before the bus had exploded, taking the driver and three other classmates' lives. The other teammates would have probably died, too, if they'd ridden the bus.

At least they'd speculated that someone had rescued Tawny-Lynn. But no one knew who'd saved her.

And no one else had survived. So how had she escaped?

"She knew more than she was telling," his father bellowed. "And no one wants her here now."

An image of a skinny, teenage girl with wheat-colored hair and enormous green eyes taunted him. Tawny-Lynn had lost her mother when she was three, had adored her sister, Peyton, and suffered her father's abuse.

"You don't know that she even wants to stay. She probably has a life somewhere else. But if she does decide to live at White Forks, that's her right."

"She doesn't give a flying fig about that property or this town. Else she wouldn't have run the way she did."

"She went to college, Dad. Besides, you could hardly blame her for leaving," Chaz said. "No one here seemed to care about her."

"You listen to me, Chaz," his father said as if Chaz were still twelve years old. "I'm not just speaking for myself. I've discussed this with the town council."

Two of the members who'd also lost girls that day served on the council now.

"That ranch is run-down," his father continued. "Just pay her a visit and tell her to sell it. Hell, I'll buy the damn property from her just to force her out."

Chaz couldn't believe that his father was so bitter. That bitterness had festered inside and turned him into a different man.

And not in a good way.

"You want me to go see her and write her a check myself?"

Chaz gritted his teeth. "No, I'll talk to her. But—" He gave his father a stern look. "I'm not going to run her off. I'll just ask her what her plans are. For all we know, she's here to hang a for-sale sign and you're in an uproar for nothing."

His father wiped a bead of perspiration from his neck. "Let me know." He strode to the door, but paused with one hand on the doorknob. "And remember what I said. If you don't get rid of her, I will."

Chaz narrowed his eyes. "That sounds like a threat, Dad."

His father shrugged. "Just thinking about the town."

He couldn't believe his father had held on to his anger for so long. "Well, don't. Leave her alone and let me do my job."

In fact, he would pay Tawny-Lynn a visit. Not to harass her, but to find out if she'd remembered anything else about the day of the crash.

Something that might help him find out what happened to their sisters.

TAWNY-LYNN SHIVERED as she climbed from her SUV and surveyed White Forks. The ranch consisted of fifty acres, just a small parcel of the original two hundred acres that had been used to breed livestock.

But her father had sold it off to make ends meet long ago, and now the barns and stables were broken down and rotting. The chicken coop had been ripped apart in a storm. The roof needed new shingles, and the grass had withered and died—only tiny patches of green poking through the dry ground.

Spring was fading into summer, the weeds choking the yard and climbing near the front porch. The big white farmhouse that she'd loved as a little girl needed painting, the porch was sagging and the shutters hung askew as if a storm had tried to rip them from the frame of the house.

As though the life had been ripped from it the day Peyton had gone missing.

Maybe before—when her mother had died. Although she hardly remembered her. She was three, Peyton five.

Their father's depression and drinking had started then and had grown worse over the years.

Somewhere she heard a dog barking, and figured it had to be a stray

A breeze stirred the leaves on the trees, echoing with voices from the past, and sending the tire swing swaying. Images of her and Peyton playing in the swing, laughing and squealing, flashed back. Snippets of other memories followed like a movie trailer—the two of them chasing the mutt they'd called Bitsy. Picking wildflowers and using them for bows in their hair.

Gathering fresh eggs from Barb and Jean, the two chickens they'd named after their favorite elementary school teachers.

Then her teenage years where she and Peyton had grown apart. Peyton and Ruth Camden had been the pretty girls, into boys, when she'd been a knobby-kneed, awkward shy tomboy.

She'd felt left out.

Then the bus crashed, and Peyton and Ruth were both gone. And her father and the entire town blamed her.

Willing away the anguish and guilt clawing at her, Tawny-Lynn started toward the house. But an engine rumbled from the dirt drive leading into the ranch, and she whipped her head around, alarmed as the sheriff's car rolled in and came to a stop.

Had the town already heard she was back and sent the sheriff to run her off?

They were pulling out all the punches before she even set foot in the house.

The sheriff cut the engine, then opened the door and a long, big body unfolded itself from the driver's side. Thick dark hair capped a tanned, chiseled face. Broad shoulders stretched tight in the man's uniform, and he removed sunglasses to reveal dark, piercing eyes beneath the brim of his Stetson.

Eyes that skated over her with a deep frown.

Her heart stuttered when she realized who the man was.

Chaz Camden.

Ruth's brother and the boy she'd had a crush on seven years ago. The boy whose family had despised her and blamed her for their loss.

The boy who'd visited her in the hospital and tried to push her to remember like everyone else.

CHAZ HADN'T BEEN to White Forks in years and was shocked at its dilapidated condition.

He was even more stunned at how much Tawny-Lynn had changed.

The wheat-colored hair was still the same, although longer and wavier than he remembered. And those grass-green eyes were just as vivid and haunted.

But the skinny teenager had developed some womanly curves that would make a man's mouth water.

"Hello, Tawny-Lynn." Damn, his voice sounded hoarse. Rough with desire. Something he hadn't felt in way too long.

And something he'd never felt for this girl... er...woman.

She shaded her eyes with her hand. "You're sheriff now?"

He gave a clipped nod. He hadn't planned on law enforcement work, but his sister's disappearance had triggered his interest. He'd wanted to find her, and it seemed the best way.

"So the town sent you to run me off?"

She had no idea how close to the truth she was. "I just heard you were here. I'm sorry for your loss."

"Don't pretend that your family and mine were friends, Chaz. I know how the town and the Camdens feel about me." She gestured to his car. "So you can go back and report that I'm here only to clean up this place so I can put it on the market. I don't intend to stick around."

Chaz heard the anger and hurt in her voice and also recognized underlying guilt. God knows, he'd blamed himself enough.

He was Ruth's big brother. He should have been able to keep her safe.

If only he'd been closer to his sister, known what was going on in her head. Some folks thought she and Peyton had run off together, maybe with boys they'd met somewhere.

But others believed they'd been kidnapped.

Tawny-Lynn turned to her SUV, raised the trunk door and reached for her suitcase. He automatically reached for it himself, and their hands touched. A frisson of something sparked between them, taking him off guard.

She must have felt it, too, because her eyes widened in alarm. "I can handle it, Chaz."

"Tawny-Lynn," he said, his voice gruff.

Her shoulders tensed. "What?"

What could he say? "I'm sorry for the way things went down back then."

Anguish flickered on her face before she masked it. "Everyone was hurting, Chaz. Grieving. In shock."

The fact that she was making excuses for the way people treated her proved she was compassionate. Still, she'd been wronged, and obviously hadn't overcome that pain.

"Did you ever remember anything else?" he asked, then immediately regretted pushing her when she dropped the suitcase and grabbed the handle.

"No. If I did, don't you think I would have told someone?"

That was the question that plagued him. Some speculated that she'd helped Ruth and Peyton run away, while others believed she'd seen the kidnapper and kept quiet out of fear.

Of course, Dr. Riggins said she had amnesia caused from the accident.

So if she had seen the kidnapper, the memory was locked in her head.

HE PULLED THE file with the photos from the bus crash from his locked desk and flipped through the pictures from the newspaper. The bus driver, fifty-nine-year-old Trevor Jergins, had died instantly when he'd crashed through the front window as the bus had careened over the ridge.

The pictures of the team were there, too. Seventeen-year-old Joan Marx, fifteen-year-old Cassie Truman and sixteen-year-old Aubrey Pullman. All players on the high school softball team.

All girls who died in that crash.

Then there was Ruth and Peyton…

And Tawny-Lynn.

She'd had a concussion and hadn't remembered anything about the accident seven years ago. Had she remembered something since?

Now that she was back in town, would she expose him for what he'd done?

No…he couldn't let that happen. If she started to cause trouble, he'd have to get rid of her.

He'd made it this long without anyone knowing. He didn't intend to go to jail now.

Chapter Two

Tawny-Lynn bounced her suitcase up the rickety porch steps, her pulse clamoring. Good heavens. She'd had a crush on Chaz Camden when she was sixteen, but she thought she'd buried those feelings long ago.

He was even more good-looking now. Those teenage muscles had developed into a powerful masculine body that had thrown her completely off guard.

He looked good in a uniform, too.

Don't go there. You have to clean this wreck of a place up and get the hell out of town.

The door screeched when she jammed the metal key in the lock and pushed it open. Dust motes rose and swirled in the hazy light streaming in through the windows, which looked like they hadn't been cleaned in a decade.

But the clutter inside was even worse. Newspapers, magazines, mail and bills overflowed the scarred oak coffee table and kitchen table. Her father had always been messy and had liked to collect junk, even to the point of buying grab bags at the salvage store, but his habit had turned into hoarding. Every conceivable space on the counter was loaded down with canned goods, boxes of assorted junk, beer cans, liquor bottles and, of all things, oversize spice containers.

Odd for a man who never cooked.

Junk boxes of nuts and bolts and screws were piled in one corner, dirty clothes had been dumped on the faded-plaid sofa, several pairs of tattered shoes were strewn about and discarded take-out containers lay haphazardly around the kitchen and den.

The sound of mice skittering somewhere in the kitchen sent a shudder through her. If the main area looked like this, she dreaded seeing the other rooms.

The stench of stale beer and liquor mingled with moldy towels and smoke.

Tawny-Lynn heaved a frustrated breath, half tempted to light a match, toss it into the pile and burn the whole place down.

But knowing her luck, she'd end up in prison for arson and the town would throw a party to celebrate her incarceration.

She refused to give them the pleasure.

But she was going to need cleaning supplies. A lot of them. Then she'd handle what repairs she could on her own, but she'd have to hire someone to take care of the major problems.

She left her suitcase in the den while she walked to the master bedroom on the main floor, glanced inside and shook her head. Her father's room was as messy as the other two rooms. More liquor bottles, papers, clothes, towels that had soured and would need to be thrown away.

Had he lived like this?

He was probably so inebriated that he didn't care.

Deciding she'd check out the upstairs before she headed into town to pick up supplies, she stepped over a muddy pair of work boots and made it to the stairwell. Cool air drifted through the eaves of the old house as she clenched the bannister. At one time her mother had kept a runner on the wooden steps, but apparently her father had ripped it out so the floors were bare now, scarred and crusted with dirt.

Bracing herself for a blast from the past, she paused at the first bedroom on the right. Peyton's room. The frilly, once bright pink, ruffled curtains still hung on the windows although they'd faded to a dull shade. But everything else in the room remained untouched. Posters from rock bands, a team banner and photographs of the team and Peyton and Ruth were still thumbtacked on the bulletin board above the white, four-poster bed. The stuffed animals and dolls she'd played with as a child stood like a shrine on the corner bookcase.

Memories of her sister pummeled her, making it difficult to breathe. She could still see the two of them playing dolls on the floor. Peyton braiding her hair in front of the antique mirror, using one of their mother's fancy pearl combs at the crown to dress up the look.

Peyton slamming the door and shutting her out, when she and Ruth wanted to be alone.

Cleaning this room would be the hardest, but it would have to be done. Although she'd feared the worst had happened to her sister over the years, that she was dead or being held hostage by some crazed maniac rapist, it still seemed wrong to discard her things, almost as if she were erasing Peyton from her life.

Or accepting that she was gone and never coming back.

Dragging herself back to the task at hand, she walked next door to her room. Her breath caught when she looked inside.

Her room had not been preserved, as Peyton's had.

In fact, someone had tossed the drawers and dresser. And on the mirror, hate words had been written in red.

Blood or lipstick, she wasn't sure.

But the message was clear just the same.

The girls' blood is on your head.

CHAZ COULDN'T ERASE the image of Tawny-Lynn from his mind as he made rounds in the small town.

He hadn't paid much attention to her when she'd tagged after his sister years ago. Had thought she had a crush on him and hadn't wanted to encourage it.

He'd been in love with Sonya Wilkerson and, that last year when Ruth had been a senior, he'd played baseball for the junior college on a scholarship that he'd planned to use to earn a forestry degree.

Then Ruth and Peyton went missing and he'd decided to pursue law enforcement and get the answers his family wanted.

Only so far he'd failed.

Maybe Tawny-Lynn would remember something now that she was back.

His phone beeped as he parked at Donna's Diner on the corner of Main Street, and he noticed the high school softball coach, Jim Wake, chatting with Mrs. Calvin. He'd kept up with the local games enough to know her daughter played for the team. The woman looked annoyed, but the coach patted her arm, using the charm he'd always used to soothe meddling, pushy parents. Everyone wanted their kid to get more play time, to be the star of the team.

If he remembered correctly, Tawny-Lynn had been damn good. Much better than her sister, although Peyton had been prettier and more of a flirt. She'd danced through dating the football team one at a time, then when spring rolled around, she'd moved on to the baseball players.

But he'd stayed clear. Peyton was his sister's best friend. Off-limits.

He parked and went inside, his stomach growling. One day he'd learn to cook, but for now Donna supplied great homemade meals at a decent price, and today's special was her famous meat loaf. She refused to give anyone the recipe or reveal her secret ingredient.

A late-spring storm was brewing, the skies darkening as the day progressed. Wind tossed dust and leaves across the asphalt, the scent of coffee, barbecue and apple pie greeting him as he entered.

The dinner crowd had already arrived, and he waved to Billy Dean and Leroy in the far corner, then noted that the parents of the three girls who'd died in the crash were sitting in a booth together, deep in conversation.

Mayor Theodore Truman, Cassie's father, seemed to be leading the discussion. The Marx couple and Aubrey Pullman's mother listened intently. Sadly, Aubrey's father had killed himself two years after the accident without even leaving a note. Rumor was that he'd grieved himself to death.

He had to walk past them to reach the only empty booth, and Mayor Truman looked up, saw him and gestured for him to stop.

"Hello, Mayor." He tipped his hat to Mr. and Mrs. Marx and Judy Pullman in greeting.

"Is it true? Tawny-Lynn Boulder is back?" Mayor Truman asked.

Chaz tensed, hating the way the man said her name as if she'd committed some heinous crime. "She's here to take care of her father's estate."

Mr. Marx stood, his anger palpable as he adjusted his suit jacket. "Your father said he talked to you."

Chaz hated small-town politics. He hated even more that his father thought he ran the town just because he had money. "Yes, he voiced his concerns."

"What are you going to do about that *woman?*" Mayor Truman asked.

Chaz planted both hands on his hips. "Ms. Boulder has every right to be here. You might show a little sympathy toward her. After all, she lost her father and, seven years ago, her sister, too."

The mayor's bushy eyebrows rose. He obviously didn't like to be put in his place. But Chaz was his own man.

He started to leave, but Judy Pullman stood and touched his hand, then leaned toward him, speaking quietly. "Sheriff, does she…remember anything about that day?"

Chaz squeezed her hand, understanding the questions still plaguing her. For God's sake, they dogged him, too. Like who had caused that freak accident.

Or had it been an accident?

They needed closure, but unfortunately their hopes lay in Tawny-Lynn's hands. A lot of pressure for her.

"No, ma'am. I know we all want answers, and

if she does remember something, trust me, I'll let everyone know."

"Is she...here to stay?"

He shook his head, thinking about how lost she looked facing that crumbling farmhouse. There had to be ghosts inside waiting for her.

"She said she's just going to clean up the ranch and put it on the market."

Mrs. Pullman stared at him for a long minute, then gave him a pained smile. "I guess I can't blame her for running."

Neither could he.

But if others still harbored as much animosity as the mayor and his father, he'd have to keep an eye out for her.

TAWNY-LYNN TUCKED the laundry list of supplies she needed into her purse and drove toward town. The road was lonely and deserted, the countryside filled with small houses interspersed between flat farmland.

A mile from town she passed the trailer park where Patti Mercer, the pitcher on her old team, used to live. Patti had dodged a bullet because of a stomach bug that day. Unlike her sister, Joy, who'd gotten pregnant at eighteen and still lived in the trailer where she'd grown up, Patti had earned a softball scholarship and had left Camden Crossing. Tawny-Lynn wondered what she was doing now.

The road curved to the right, and she wove

around a deserted tractor. The town square hadn't changed except they'd refurbished the playground in the park, and the storefronts had been redesigned to resemble an old Western town. The tack shop had expanded, a fabric store had been added near the florist, the library now adjoined city hall and the sheriff's office had been painted and bore a new sign.

She passed the sheriff's office and the diner, then saw the general store and decided they'd probably have everything she needed. If not, Hank's Hardware would. But she wasn't ready to tackle repairs. She had to start by scraping off the layers of dirt and grime.

She pulled into a parking spot, noting that the diner was crowded. A couple who looked familiar, but one she couldn't quite place, exited the general store as she entered.

She grabbed a cart, then strolled the aisles, filling it with industrial-size cleaner, Pine-Sol, scrub brushes, dish soap, laundry detergent, dusting spray and polish, glass cleaner, then threw in a new broom and mop along with buckets, sponges and a duster with an extended handle so she could reach the corners.

Thankfully she'd checked her father's supply shed and had been surprised to find buckets and boxes full of tools of every kind. Apparently tools were another aspect of his hoarding. He could have opened his own hardware business from the shed out back.

A couple with a toddler walked by, the baby bab-bling as he rode on his father's back. She frowned, her heart tugging a little. She hadn't thought about having her own family, hadn't been able to let any man in her life.

But this guy looked familiar. Maybe he'd been in her class?

She continued past them with her head averted. She didn't intend to be here long enough to renew friendships or start new ones.

The locals probably wouldn't welcome her any-way.

She bent to choose some oven cleaner, then added it to the cart, but as she stood, she bumped into a body. She twisted to apologize then looked up to see an older woman with thinning gray hair staring at her.

She frowned, trying to place her.

"Are you Tawny-Lynn Boulder?" the woman asked.

Tawny-Lynn swallowed. "Yes."

"You probably don't know me but my name is Evelyn Jergins. My husband drove the bus for the softball team. He died that day in the crash."

Tawny-Lynn's heart clenched. "Oh, I'm sorry."

The woman narrowed her eyes. "You— They said you might know what made him wreck."

The urge to run slammed into Tawny-Lynn.

"No.... I'm so sorry, but I still don't remember much about that day."

"Well, that's too bad. Trevor was a good man. I miss him every day."

"I miss my sister, too," Tawny-Lynn said.

"I heard about your daddy. That's too bad."

Tawny-Lynn shrugged, touched by the woman's sincerity. "I came back to clean up the ranch and sell it."

"Then you're not moving back?"

She shook her head. "No, I live in Austin."

She arched her brows. "Really? Are you married?"

"No." God, no. She hadn't been involved with anyone since her freshmen year in college when she'd found her boyfriend cheating on her. He'd blamed her. Said she wouldn't really let him in. That she was closed off emotionally.

Maybe she was. The nightmares of the past tormented her at night.

She quickly said goodbye, grabbed her cart and headed to the front. A silver-haired woman with tortoiseshell glasses was working the checkout counter and smiled as Tawny-Lynn unloaded the cart.

"Looks like you got a job ahead of you, hon."

Tawny-Lynn forced a smile, although she dreaded the backbreaking job. "Yes, I do."

She didn't offer more information, and thankfully another customer came up behind her and the woman tallied her items quickly. Tawny-Lynn paid with her debit card and headed outside, but as she loaded the items into her trunk, she sensed someone watching her, and anxiety tightened her shoulders.

When she turned, Cassie Truman's father was standing behind her. Age lines fanned his face, his hair had streaks of gray, but he still carried himself as if he were superior to everyone else.

"Mr. Truman," she said, remembering the way he'd banned her from his daughter's funeral.

"I'm the mayor now."

So he and Chaz's father must be buddy-buddy, both in control of the town.

She reached to close the trunk of her SUV. "Excuse me, I need to leave."

"*Are* you leaving?" he said.

Anger shot through her at his tone. The Camdens and the parents of the girls who'd died blamed her for not remembering details of that day, but she couldn't help it.

It was like a black hole had swallowed her memory of that day. She wanted the memories back, wanted to know how she'd escaped the bus with a broken leg and where Ruth and Peyton were.

But no amount of pushing or counseling had helped. She'd even tried hypnosis, but that had failed as well.

"As soon as I put the ranch up for sale," she said, a trace of bitterness in her tone.

"You still aren't going to tell us what happened back then?"

Pain, sharp and raw, splintered her. "Believe me, *Mayor* Truman, if I ever remember, the town will know."

Battling tears, she brushed past him, jumped in the SUV and backed away.

Her hands were shaking, her heart racing. Damn him. Damn her.

She wanted to remember and put the story to rest.

She slapped the steering wheel and brushed away tears. She had lost her sister that day, too.

Night had set in, the Friday-night diner crowd filing outside to their cars and heading home. She wondered if they still played bingo at the church and had monthly dances at the rec.

Not that she would be attending any. She meant what she'd said. She'd clean up White Forks and get the hell out before the town destroyed her again.

Her SUV hit a pothole, and she braked, then slowed as she drove the country road. Seconds later, lights appeared behind her, and she checked her rearview mirror, anxious as the car sped up and rode her bumper.

Irritated, she braked again, hoping the driver would pass her, but the jerk slowed slightly, then continued to ride her as she left town. The curve caught her off guard, and she skimmed the edge of the road, then the car passed, forcing her toward the ditch.

Sweat beaded on her hands as she clenched the steering wheel and tried to maintain control, but her tires hit another pothole, and the Jeep skidded off the road.

Her body slammed against the steering wheel as the SUV pitched forward, the front bumper ramming into the ditch.

The impact jerked her neck, her head hit the back of the seat and the world went dark.

Chapter Three

Chaz paid his bill at the diner, then checked in with his deputy, Ned Lemone, a young, restless guy who'd taken the job but made it clear he wanted to move to a big city and make detective. Not enough action around Camden Crossing.

At least he didn't mind the night shift.

"Anything I need to know about?" Chaz asked.

Deputy Lemone shook his head. "A domestic out at the Cooter farm."

"Wally and Inez at it again?"

His deputy nodded. "She threw a cast-iron skillet at him. Broke his big toe."

Chaz shook his head. The couple fought like cats and dogs, but refused to separate. He'd been out there a half dozen times himself.

Chaz walked to the door. "Call me if anything comes up."

Deputy Lemone nodded, and Chaz strode outside, went to his car and drove toward his cabin a couple of miles outside town on a creek, only three miles from White Forks.

And on the opposite side of town from his folks. Maybe *he* should relocate even farther away from them.

But he'd stayed, hoping being close might lead him to a clue about Ruth's disappearance.

He wound around the curve on the deserted road, fighting thoughts of Tawny-Lynn when he noticed a battered, blue SUV had nose-dived into the ditch.

Tawny-Lynn's SUV.

Dammit.

He swerved to the side of the road, threw the cruiser into Park and jogged over to her Jeep. His boots skidded on gravel as he rushed down the incline.

He glanced inside the driver's side and saw Tawny-Lynn raise her head and look up at him. Blood dotted her forehead, and she seemed dazed and confused.

He pulled the door open. "Tawny-Lynn, are you all right?"

She nodded, then touched her forehead. He did a quick assessment. Her seat belt must have kept her from serious harm, but the Jeep was so old it didn't have air bags.

"What happened?" Chaz asked as he lifted her chin to examine her for other injuries. The cut was small, and he didn't think it needed stitches, but she could have a concussion.

"I... A car came up behind me," she said, her voice hoarse. "I slowed to let him go past but he kept riding my bumper. And when he passed me, he was so close I ran off the road."

"Did the driver stop?"

She shook her head. "No, he raced on by. He seemed like he was in real hurry."

"Did you see who was driving?"

"No."

"But you said 'he.' You're sure it was a man?"

She dropped her hands to her lap. "No. The car had tinted windows."

"What kind of car was it?"

Tawny-Lynn shrugged. "I don't know, Chaz. It was dark and the lights nearly blinded me." She reached for her keys. "Do you think you can help me get out of here?"

"Sure. But I'm going to call a medic to check you out. You might have a concussion."

"I'm fine," Tawny-Lynn said. "I just want to go back to the ranch."

He grabbed the keys from her. "You're not driving until you're examined by a professional."

She glared at him. "Chaz, please—"

"It would be irresponsible of me to let you drive when you might have a head injury." He grabbed his phone from his belt and made the call.

"Racine, there was an accident on White Forks Road. Send the medics out here now." A pause. "Yeah, thanks." He disconnected then punched the number for Henry's Auto Repair. "Henry, can you send a tow truck out to White Forks Road? A car accident, Jeep in a ditch that needs pulling out."

"Sure. I'm on my way," Henry said.

Chaz disconnected, his chest tightening as he glanced down at Tawny-Lynn. Her face looked pale in the moonlight, and she was rubbing her chest as if she might have cracked a rib.

He didn't like the fact that she'd had an accident the very day she'd come to town. Or the fact that the driver had left her in the ditch.

Had it been an accident or had someone intentionally run her off the road?

TAWNY-LYNN STRUGGLED to remember details about the car. The driver was probably some joyriding teenager, or maybe a drunk driver.

But the message on her mirror at home taunted her.

Someone didn't want her here. Actually a lot of people didn't want her here. Had one of them run her into that ditch to get rid of her?

She unfastened her seat belt and started to climb from the car, but Chaz took her arm and helped her out. For a moment she was dizzy, but he steadied her and the world righted itself.

"You are hurt," he said in a gruff voice.

"I've been through worse," she said, then immediately regretted her comment when his gaze locked with hers. They both knew she'd barely survived that crash. Although no one knew how she'd escaped the burning vehicle.

Chaz started to say something, but the sound of a siren wailing rent the air, and red lights twirled in the night sky as the ambulance approached. A second later, the tow truck rolled in on its heels, and Tawny-Lynn had to succumb to an exam by the paramedics.

Meanwhile, Chaz spoke with Henry, the fifty-something owner of the auto repair shop, and supervised as the man towed her Jeep from the ditch.

"Your blood pressure's a little high, miss," the blond medic said.

"Wouldn't you think that's normal after an accident?" she said wryly.

He nodded, then listened to her heart while the other medic cleaned her forehead and applied a small butterfly bandage.

"Heart sounds okay," the medic said. He used a penlight and examined her eyes, instructing her to follow the light.

"I'm really fine," Tawny-Lynn said. "I was wearing my seat belt so I didn't hit the windshield."

"How about the steering wheel?"

She nodded. "My chest did, but nothing is broken." She had suffered broken ribs in the bus accident and knew that kind of breath-robbing pain.

"We should take you in for X-rays."

Tawny-Lynn shook her head. "No need. I told you, I'm fine."

The medics exchanged looks as Chaz approached. "If you won't go in, you need to sign a waiver, miss."

"Then let me sign it. I just want to go home." Not that she considered White Forks home anymore. But she didn't like people hovering over her.

She'd had too much of that after the bus wreck. Of course, the hovering had been people demanding that she remember, pressuring her, wanting answers that she couldn't give.

"Maybe you should go to the hospital for observation," Chaz suggested.

She'd been taking care of herself far too long to welcome attention, especially from Chaz Camden.

"I don't need a hospital," she said. "It was just a little accident."

The medic handed her a form attached to a clipboard, and she gave them her autograph.

They packed up and left just as Henry finished dragging her SUV from the ditch. The thing was old and beat up, so a bent fender with a little body damage didn't faze her. Not as long as the car would run.

"You shouldn't drive it until I check it out," Henry said. "Front end probably needs realignment. And that back tire is as bald as a baby's butt."

"How long will it take to replace the tire and check the alignment?"

"Day or two. I can call you when I'm done."

Tawny-Lynn hedged. She didn't have a lot of

money, but she also didn't want to get stranded on her way back to Austin. And her father's old pickup was at the ranch, so she'd have transportation. "All right."

"I'll give you a lift home," Chaz offered.

She didn't want to be in the same car with Chaz—to share the same air—because he smelled too good, too darn masculine.

Sexy.

And whether or not she wanted to admit it, she was shaken by the accident and would love to lean on him.

But she couldn't allow herself to do that.

She grabbed her purse from the Jeep, then removed one of her business cards with her phone number on it. "Call me when you have it ready."

By the time she finished talking to Henry, Chaz had unloaded her supplies and stowed them in the trunk of his squad car.

Henry waved to her, then jumped in the tow truck and chugged away, pulling her Jeep behind him, the clank of metal echoing as he disappeared from sight.

"He'll give you a fair price," Chaz said as if he sensed her concerns about money.

She didn't comment. Instead she walked around to the passenger side of his car and climbed in. The world was spinning again, the seconds before she'd slammed into the ditch taking her back seven years.

She massaged her temple, but the sound of screams and crying reverberated in her head.

"Tawny-Lynn," Chaz said softly. "Are you sure you're all right?" He closed his hand over hers, and her fingers tingled with awareness, unsettling her even more. She desperately wanted to hold on to him. To have someone assure her that things would be all right.

"Yes, I'm fine," she said.

BUT NOTHING WAS all right. She was all alone. Everyone in Camden Crossing hated her, and the only way to fix that was to remember what had happened that day.

Chaz gave her a sympathetic look, then started the car and drove to White Forks. The woods backing up to the ranch seemed darker and more ominous tonight. Chaz maneuvered the dirt drive, avoiding the worst potholes, then parked in front of the house.

Somewhere in the distance, she heard an animal rustling in dry leaves as she climbed out. Then the howl of a coyote as if it was close by.

Chaz opened the trunk and lifted one of the boxes, and she grabbed two bags of supplies and led the way up the steps. But when she touched the doorknob to unlock the door, it swung open.

Chaz immediately pressed a hand across her chest to stop her from entering. "Did you lock it when you left?"

She nodded, remembering the bloody message on her mirror.

Was someone inside now?

CHAZ'S INSTINCTS SNAPPED to full alert. He set the box on the porch, removed his weapon and scanned the front of the property. He hadn't seen anyone pulling up, and there were no cars in sight.

Still, the door was unlocked, and on the heels of Tawny-Lynn's so-called accident, that raised his suspicions.

"Chaz?"

He pressed a finger to his lips to shush her, then motioned for her to stay behind him. He inched inside, looking left then right, shocked at the stacks of papers and junk filling every nook and cranny of the living room and kitchen.

The stench of stale beer and liquor mingled with mold, and gave him an understanding of the mammoth amount of trash bags and cleaning supplies Tawny-Lynn had bought.

It had been years since he'd been in the house and tried to remember the layout. The master bedroom was on the main floor, the girls' rooms upstairs.

The floor creaked as Tawny-Lynn followed behind him, and he veered to the left into the master suite. It was just as nasty and cluttered as the front rooms.

But no one was inside.

"I don't hear anything," Tawny-Lynn whispered.

Neither did he, but a predator could be hiding in a closet or upstairs, ready to attack. He slowly closed his hand around the bedroom closet doorknob and yanked it open, his gun raised. It was empty except for the stacks of old shoes, hats and clothing.

"Stay here while I check the upstairs."

"No, I'm going with you," Tawny-Lynn whispered.

He gave her a sharp look, then decided maybe it was best if she did follow him, in case the intruder was hiding in the storage shed outside. He didn't want to leave her alone.

They crossed back through the room, then he tiptoed up the steps, but the wooden boards creaked beneath his weight. The first room was Peyton's, still decorated like it had been years ago. For a moment, grief hit him as an image of Ruth sitting cross-legged on Peyton's bed flashed in front of his eyes.

Heaving a breath to refocus, he yanked open the closet door, but all he found were Peyton's clothes. Jeans and T-shirts, a prom dress.

The softball cleats gave him another pain in his chest. No wonder the parents of the three girls who'd died couldn't forget.

No one should have to bury a child.

He kept his gun poised as he pivoted, Tawny-Lynn's choppy breathing echoing behind him as he entered the hall and inched to her room.

He paused at the doorway, anger bolting through him at the sight of the mirror.

"What the hell?"

"That was there when I first arrived," Tawny-Lynn whispered.

He swung around to her. "What? Why didn't you tell me?"

Tawny-Lynn shrugged. "I had no idea how long it had been there."

Chaz cursed, then strode forward to examine it. He studied the writing, then took a sniff. "Looks like blood but it's dry, so no smell. I'll take samples and send to the crime lab."

Tawny-Lynn nodded, then he stepped inside the bathroom and cursed again. "Was this here, too?"

Her eyes widened in shock as she entered. Then she shook her head in denial.

Chaz was disgusted at the sight.

The walls were covered in more blood. Fresh blood.

Whoever had broken in had written another message on the walls.

We don't want you here.
Leave or die.

THE SHERIFF WAS inside Boulder's house with the girl. Dammit to hell and back.

Chaz asked too many questions. He just wouldn't

give up investigating his sister's disappearance and the bus wreck that had taken those girls' lives.

Why couldn't he let it go?

It was over. Years ago.

But now Tawny-Lynn was back.

What if she remembered something while she was in town? What if she remembered *him?*

His *face?* That he'd been there?

No, Tawny-Lynn had sustained a head injury that had robbed those memories, wiped them out and given her a clean slate. She couldn't remember now.

If she did, she'd have to die.

Chapter Four

Chaz studied the bathroom, his anger mounting. Tawny-Lynn hadn't done anything to earn this kind of abusive treatment. Not certain he believed her earlier statement about the message, he pressed her again. "Why didn't you call when you found that first message?"

Tawny-Lynn shrugged. "I know you and your family hate me."

"I'm not my family," Chaz said. "I'm the law, and no one is harassed or threatened on my watch without me taking it seriously."

Tawny-Lynn averted her eyes as if she didn't know how to respond.

"I'm going to take samples and look for prints."

"In here or all through the house?"

He grimaced as he considered the question. "I'll start in here."

"With all this dust and clutter, it would probably be a nightmare to do every room."

She was right. "I'll check the doors and major

surfaces. But it'll take me a while. Let me grab my kit from the car."

"Okay. I'll bring in the rest of the cleaning supplies."

"I'll give you a hand. But I'd rather you not clean anything until I look around."

He followed her down the stairs, noting how fragile and tired she looked. No telling what time she'd gotten up this morning, and then she'd driven for hours and walked into this disaster.

It took them three trips to bring everything inside. Chaz retrieved his kit and decided to check the doors and kitchen first, so Tawny-Lynn could at least clean up the kitchen enough to prepare a meal or make coffee in the morning.

She watched him as he shined a flashlight along the doorway and kitchen counter and took a couple of prints on the back doorknob and screen. There was so much dust on the piles of newspapers and table that he didn't see any prints. Besides, there would have been no reason for the intruder to touch the empty liquor and beer bottles Boulder had thrown into the heap in the corner

"I'm done in here if you want to start cleaning this room while I'm upstairs."

"Thanks. I don't think I could eat anything in this house until it's fumigated."

He chuckled. "Your father obviously never threw anything away."

"Or took out the garbage." She grabbed a trash

bag and began to sort the cans and bottles into one bag for recycling, while he headed to the stairs.

He yanked on gloves and set to work. On the chance that the intruder hadn't worn gloves and had touched the railing, he examined it, found a print and lifted it. Then he realized it was probably Tawny-Lynn's and asked for a sample of hers for elimination purposes when he sent the others to the lab.

Upstairs, he scraped off a sample of the blood on the dresser mirror and dusted the gilded frame, but found nothing. Then he moved to the bathroom and checked the sink's countertop, but if someone had touched it, they'd wiped it clean.

He took a generous sampling of the blood on the wall, hoping to learn something from it. Was it human blood?

He photographed the writing, then took pictures of the message on the mirror, as well. Maybe a handwriting expert could analyze it. And if he had a suspect, he could compare samples. The dot over the *i* in the world *Die* had a curly tip. The writing also slanted downward at an angle and looked as if someone had jabbed at the wall out of anger.

He paused in the bedroom, his mind ticking as he wondered how the intruder had known this room was Tawny-Lynn's. It was certainly not as frilly as Peyton's, and there were dozens of sports posters on the wall, but no nameplate or picture of Tawny-Lynn to give it away. A plain navy comforter covered the antique iron bed, a teddy bear and rag doll sat on the bookshelf above a sea of mystery books, and CDs were stacked in a CD holder by a scarred pine desk.

Which suggested that the intruder had known the family well enough to know which room belonged to her.

And that he or she might have been in the house before.

TAWNY-LYNN RAKED trash and old food off the kitchen counter and into the garbage bag. She'd already filled up three bags and was going to need a truck to haul away the junk once she finished with the house.

Exhaustion pulled at her shoulders, a headache pulsing behind her eyes. a result of the accident she assumed. Or maybe it was due to the mounds of dust in the house.

She'd have to stock up on her allergy medication.

Carrying that bag out the back door, her gaze scanned the woods beyond. Was the person who'd left her those vile messages hiding out now, watching her? Hoping she'd flee the town as she had seven years ago?

"I don't want to be in Camden Crossing any more than you want me here," she muttered.

"Who are you talking to?"

Tawny-Lynn startled and spun around. Chaz

stood in the kitchen doorway, his hand covering the gun at his waist. "Did you see someone out here?"

She shook her head, silently berating herself. "No, I was talking to myself."

His eyes darkened as he studied her. "Are you sure you don't have a concussion?"

"I'm just exhausted," she admitted. "But I'm not going to bed until this kitchen is clean, so you can go home if you're finished."

"Actually I came down for a bucket and bleach."

She frowned. "What for?"

"To clean the blood off your wall and mirror."

"That's not necessary, Chaz. You've done enough already." In fact, it felt too good to have him here. Made her feel safe. Secure. Needy.

She couldn't lean on him or anyone else.

"I'll do it once I finish with the kitchen."

"No way," he said gruffly. "I don't intend to leave you here with that disgusting threat in your room, especially after you were in an accident."

God, his voice sounded almost protective. Odd, when years ago he'd hated her just like everyone else.

He didn't wait for a reply. He rummaged through the boxes of supplies, grabbed a bucket, a container of bleach and a sponge and strode back toward the stairs.

Tawny-Lynn sighed shakily and rushed back inside, but the wind whistling through the trees unnerved her and she slammed the door. Maybe it was better if Chaz was here, acting as the sheriff, of course, just in case the intruder had stuck around.

Her adrenaline kicked in, and she finished scraping off the counters, chairs, table and floors of junk, carefully stowing any unpaid bills she located, and there were dozens, into a basket on the counter. Next, she tackled the refrigerator, not surprised to find it virtually empty except for condiments that had expired, something moldy growing in a jar, a jug of sour milk and a carton of outdated eggs.

Next she tossed a rusted can opener, a toaster that was so crusted with grime that she doubted she could ever clean it, then dish towels that were mildewed.

When she finished with that, she pulled out the bleach and industrial cleaner and scoured the sink, counter and the inside and outside of the refrigerator. The counters were worn, but after several layers of crud had been removed they were passable. Other things might need to be replaced.

That is, unless she just decided to sell the ranch as it was. Maybe that was best. She didn't have money to invest in the house. The property held the real value. Whoever bought the ranch could tear down the house and build a new one or remodel this one the way they chose.

By the time she finished and mopped the floor, her body was aching for sleep. Footsteps sounded, and Chaz appeared, his big body filling the doorway.

She was filthy, sweaty and covered in dirt, while

he looked so handsome and strong that he stole the breath from her.

"You look like you're about to fall over," he said.

Tawny-Lynn leaned against the counter. At least it smelled better in this room. "It's been a long day. A good night's sleep will work wonders." Although truthfully, she hadn't had a good night's sleep in nearly a decade.

The nightmares dogged her every time she closed her eyes.

TAWNY-LYNN SWAYED, and Chaz caught her by the arm. "Exhausted? You're dizzy."

"It's just the cleaning fumes," she said, her voice strained. "I have allergies."

He nodded, unconvinced. "I'm going to send Jimmy James out here tomorrow to install new locks on the house. Dead bolts, too."

"I can take care of it," Tawny-Lynn said.

"Don't argue." Chaz gestured toward the mess in the living room. "You have your hands full already."

She rubbed her forehead, then looked up at him warily. "Why are you helping me, Chaz? I thought you hated me just like your folks and the rest of the town."

Chaz's chest tightened at her directness. He wanted to tell her that he didn't hate her, that he regretted the way he'd treated her after Ruth had disappeared, that he'd shouldered his own share of guilt and had been desperate for answers to satisfy his father.

But there was no way he could get personal with her. Revealing the truth would make him vulnerable. And he had to focus.

One day he would find his sister. That was all that mattered.

So he kept the conversation on a professional level. "I'm the sheriff, I'm just doing my job."

Something akin to disappointment flared in her big green eyes. "Of course. Well, thanks for the ride home and for cleaning the walls."

He nodded. "I'll let you know if I find a hit on any of the prints or the blood samples."

Tawny-Lynn led him to the front door, but he hung there, hesitant to leave. She looked so small and fragile. Vulnerable.

She'd been here less than twenty-four hours and already had an accident, which could have been intentional, and an intruder in her house who'd left vile threats against her.

Tawny-Lynn held the door edge, and offered him a brave smile. "Well, even if you are just doing your job, I appreciate it, Chaz. I know how the locals feel about me. I…just wish I could give them what they want."

He narrowed his eyes, pained at the sorrow in her tone. "You suffered, too. You lost your sister. People should have been more sensitive to that."

She shrugged, but the effort didn't meet her eyes.

He had the sudden impulse to reach up and pull her against him. To hold her and assure her that everything would be all right. That she'd done all she could, just as he had.

But touching her would be wrong. Would make it more difficult to keep his distance and do his job.

And his job was to keep her safe and to find the person who'd threatened her.

So he handed her his business card, told her to call him if she needed anything, then headed to his car, determined to ignore the pull of attraction between them.

TAWNY-LYNN WATCHED Chaz leave with mixed feelings. As long as he'd been in the house, she could chase away the monsters.

But when she was left alone in the house, the ghosts seeped from the walls to haunt her.

For a moment she couldn't breathe. The familiar panic attacks she'd suffered after the bus accident threatened. Willing herself to be strong, she closed her eyes and took slow, even breaths.

It had been seven years. She was alive. She was safe.

Or was she?

Judging from the bloody message on her mirror and walls, someone didn't want her here.

A shudder coursed up her body and she locked the door, then shoved a chair in front of it. The chair wouldn't keep an intruder out, but at least if it fell over, it might wake her.

If she ever managed to fall asleep.

Dusty and grimy from the work she'd done and achy from the earlier nosedive into the ditch, she forced herself to leave the chaotic mess waiting in the living room, grabbed a bottle of cleaner for the shower and climbed the stairs. She'd tackle the den tomorrow.

Chaz had erased the message from the mirror, but the ugly words still taunted her. She stripped the sheets, found clean ones in the closet and put them on the bed. Then she retrieved her toiletry bag and walked into the bathroom.

The walls smelled of bleach, but the shower looked grungy, so she scrubbed it, then the toilet and sink. Then she turned on the water, stripped and climbed in the shower. The hot water felt heavenly on her aching muscles, and she soaped and washed her body and hair, then rinsed off. She wrapped a towel around her damp hair, then stepped from the shower and brushed her teeth twice to get rid of the dust in her mouth.

She towel dried her hair, slipped on a pair of pajamas, took a sleeping pill and fell into bed. Seconds later, she closed her eyes and drifted off.

But even as she faded into sleep, images of the bloody message flashed back.

If she didn't leave town, would the intruder come back and kill her?

Chapter Five

Chaz hesitated before driving away from White Forks, but he couldn't stay with Tawny-Lynn around the clock.

Could he?

If the threats continued, he'd have to.

He carried the blood samples and prints he'd collected to the sheriff's office. His deputy was on the phone when he walked in.

Judging from the goofy grin on his face, he was talking to his girlfriend, Sheila.

He looked up at Chaz and dropped his feet from the desk. "Listen, honey, I've gotta go. Call you later."

He hung up, then quirked his brows at Chaz. "I didn't expect you back tonight."

"There was some trouble out at White Forks."

"You mean that place where the Boulder broad lives?"

"She hasn't lived there in years, but yes, that's the one. She came back to town to get her old man's ranch ready to sell."

"I heard folks around here don't much like her."

Chaz scowled at his deputy. "Who've you been listening to, Ned?"

"No one in particular. Some old women were gossiping about her in the diner. Said if she'd spoken up about what happened that day, they might have tracked down your sister and Peyton Boulder." He scratched the back of his neck. "Hell, someone even said that she helped them run off."

Chaz silently cursed. Ned had come from a neighboring town and had formed his opinions based on rumors. "First of all, I don't think my sister just ran off. She wouldn't have done that. Second, Tawny-Lynn almost died in that crash herself. She was unconscious when the paramedics found her, had a broken leg and a concussion."

Ned made a clicking sound with his teeth. "The concussion caused her amnesia?"

"Yes, according to the doctor," Chaz said.

"But the accident— Didn't the sheriff think that was suspicious?"

Chaz nodded. "There were skid marks from another vehicle on the pavement, but it started raining and they couldn't get a good print."

"Why would someone run the bus off the road?"

"Good question. The bus was carrying the softball team. Could have been some teen following too close or—"

"Competitors from another team?"

"I don't think so. The sheriff looked into each

of the girl's lives, but none of them had any serious enemies."

"So what's your theory?" Ned asked.

Chaz contemplated the file he had at home. How many times had he studied the damn thing for answers?

"I don't know. Two girls went missing from Sunset Mesa before the Camden incident and were never found. A lot of people think that a serial kidnapper took them. It's possible he was stalking one of the girls on the team and caused the accident, then kidnapped Ruth and Peyton."

"He'd have to be strong to wrestle both girls."

"Not if he had a gun, or if they were hurt in the crash."

His deputy studied his fingernails. "Do you have any idea who this guy is?"

Chaz shook his head. "No, and that's just a theory. No proof."

"But you all think that Tawny-Lynn Boulder saw this guy that day?"

"Some people think that. Like I said, she was unconscious when the medics arrived. But somehow she got out of the bus before it caught fire. Considering the fact that she had a broken leg and head injury, it's not likely she walked."

"Meaning someone dragged her to safety. But if it was the kidnapper, why not take her, too?"

"Maybe he was fixated on Ruth or Peyton. And like I said, Tawny-Lynn had a broken leg." He gritted his teeth. Depending on what the sick bastard's plans were, he probably hadn't wanted her with the injury.

"Anyway," Chaz continued. "Tonight someone left a bloody threat for Tawny-Lynn at White Forks. I took samples and managed to lift a few prints. Call the courier to pick it up, take it back to the lab and analyze it."

"Sure."

Chaz took a form from the desk and filled out the paperwork for chain of custody. "Tell the lab to call me as soon as they get the results."

The deputy narrowed his eyes as he examined the photograph of the bloody message. "Someone really wants her gone."

"It looks that way." Chaz headed back to the door. "But it's our job to protect her, Deputy. And to find out who made that threat."

TAWNY-LYNN GRIPPED the bat with sweaty palms. It was the bottom of the ninth and the Camden Cats were one run behind. The team was depending on her.

The pitcher threw a curve ball that came in low, and she barely managed to check her swing in time before the umpire called ball one.

Two more pitches and she'd tipped the ball twice. Her stomach felt jittery. Her chest hurt. She couldn't strike out now.

Another ball and it nearly hit her shoulder. She

jumped back, the ball whizzing by her head. She stepped aside to steady herself, then ground the bat at the base and raised it, ready.

The pitcher wound up as the crowd and her teammates chanted her name. A second later, she swung at the ball. Metal connected with it, sending the ball flying, and she took off running as the ball soared over the fence. Her teammates screamed in excitement, the crowd roared and Peyton, who was on second base, sailed around the bases. Tawny-Lynn was faster than her sister and nearly caught her as they raced into home plate.

Her homerun sent the team one point ahead.

Roars and cheers from the crowd echoed in her ears as Ruth stepped up to bat. Three straight swings though and she struck out.

Still, the Cats had won. The girls rushed her, clapping and shouting and hugging. The coach pounded her on the back. "You're our hero today, T!"

She beamed a smile as they grabbed their gym bags and jogged toward the bus. More congratulations and pats as the girls clamored into their seats.

"I have to stop by the bank. Let's meet up at the pizza parlor to celebrate," Coach Wake announced. He made his way back to his car while the bus driver fired up the bus.

Tawny-Lynn settled into a seat by herself while Peyton jumped in beside Ruth, and they started whispering and giggling.

Peyton was boy crazy, and Ruth was interested in someone, but they were keeping it a secret, talking in hushed voices. Jealousy sparked her to glare at them, but her sister pulled Ruth closer and tucked their heads together to shut her out.

The bus chugged around a curve, but it was dark on the country road, a storm brewing, thunder rumbling. A car raced up behind the bus and rammed it, and the bus jolted forward. The driver shouted, then tires screeched and the bus swerved toward the embankment. The ridge loomed below, and fear shot through Tawny-Lynn.

She hated heights. Had always been scared on the switchbacks.

The bus jerked again, something scraped the side, then the bus went into a skid. One of the girls screamed, brakes squealed, then the bus flew out of control, slammed into the metal guardrail and careened over the ridge.

Backpacks and gym bags slid onto the floor, and she gripped the seat edge to keep from falling. Bodies fell into the aisle, blood was flying, and she was thrown against the metal seat top as the bus crashed into the ravine.

Sometime later, she roused. It was dark, so dark...pain throbbed through her chest and leg.

She couldn't move. It was deathly quiet.

Then she felt hands pulling at her, moving her. She tried to open her eyes, but the world was foggy.

Breathing rasped around her. She tried to see

*who was pulling her from the bus, but it was too
dark. Then she heard crying again—another
scream. Voices.*

Was her sister all right?

*She struggled to see, but...there was a man...his
face...hidden in shadows. Who was he?*

Tawny-Lynn jerked awake, panting for a breath.
The dream...had been so real. A memory.

She had heard a voice. Seen a face.

A man's? A woman's? Peyton's maybe?

God help her, who was it?

CHAZ POPPED OPEN a cold beer when he made it
home, his mind obsessing over Tawny-Lynn. Was
she sleeping now? Or was she awake, terrified the
person who'd left her that bloody message would
return and make good on his threat?

Tension knotted his shoulders. He wanted to be
back at White Forks watching out for her. Making
sure she was safe.

Holding her...

Dammit, no. Tawny-Lynn was the last woman
on earth he needed to be attracted to.

Why her?

Why now?

Life would be so much simpler if she cleaned that
place up quickly, hung the for-sale sign, left town
and never came back.

Then he wouldn't have to think about her being

on that deserted run-down ranch by herself where God knew anyone could sneak up and attack her.

It wasn't as if she didn't have enemies. She had too many to count.

The people who'd lost family members in that crash despised her for not being able to give them closure by identifying the person who'd hit the bus and caused the crash.

Their family members, Coach Wake and half the town had also been questioned as suspects and resented it because Tawny-Lynn could have cleared their names.

Coach Wake has literally sobbed at the news of the crash, saying maybe if he'd been with the girls on the bus he could have done something to save them. Instead, he'd driven his own car, taken a side road, then stopped for cash and a surprise cake to take to the celebration dinner.

Tawny-Lynn's delicate face flashed in Chaz's head, and he grimaced, sipped his beer and headed to his home office. The cabin was small, but he'd carved a workspace in the second bedroom where he'd hung a gigantic whiteboard and laid out everything he knew about the missing girls from Sunset Mesa and Camden Crossing.

A smaller board held photos of other missing young women from various states for comparison purposes so he could look for connections.

Once again, he studied the pictures former sheriff Harold Simmons had taken of the accident. The bus was a mess, dented and crushed against a boulder in the ravine, flames shooting from all sides.

Keith Plumbing, a local handyman had driven up on the scene and called it in. His statement said he'd first seen smoke, then stopped and realized it was a bus and called 911. He'd run down the embankment to rescue the students trapped inside, but by the time he reached the bus, it burst into flames. He saw Tawny-Lynn lying in the dirt several feet away. But no one else was around.

Due to the fact that Keith called in the accident and had a history of drinking on the job, and he'd worked in Camden Crossing and Sunset Mesa, the sheriff questioned him as a person of interest. Plumbing could have caused the crash, then lied about the timing, dragged Tawny-Lynn out to safety but couldn't save the others.

Although he'd sworn he hadn't seen Peyton or Ruth. And if he'd hurt them or kidnapped them, where had he taken them? He hadn't had enough time between the time of the crash and when he'd called in the accident to dispose of a body.

Another photograph showed Tawny-Lynn unconscious on the stretcher, her leg twisted, blood streaking her face and hands. She looked so pale and fragile that he wondered how she'd survived.

Shaking off emotions he didn't want to feel for her, he glanced at the list of suspects the sheriff had considered. Plumbing had been one. He'd also questioned Barry Dothan, a young man with a mental disability that affected his learning and behavior.

Dothan liked to watch teenagers and took pictures of them on the track, swim team and softball field. But his mother swore that Barry was harmless, that he would never hurt a soul. The pictures of Ruth and Peyton posted on the corkboard above his bed were the only evidence that incriminated him. Some of the girls at school claimed they felt uncomfortable around him, but none of them had accused him of inappropriate behavior.

Chaz downed the rest of his beer and grabbed another, pacing to calm himself. God, his heart hurt just imagining what might have happened to his sister and Ruth.

He skimmed the former sheriff's notes. The investigators they'd called in from the county had found remains of three girls and the driver in the ashes left after the bus had exploded.

Ruth and Peyton were not among them.

So what the hell had happened to them?

Could Plumbing have had more time than they'd originally thought, time to kill the girls and dump their bodies somewhere?

They'd searched the man's truck. No girls, blood or forensics inside.

They'd also combed the area surrounding the crash site for bodies, a dead end as well.

Dothan didn't seem smart enough to abduct two girls and hide them.

But nobody else was there.

There had to be, though—or else how had Tawny-Lynn escaped the burning bus?

Peyton or Ruth could have dragged her out. But then what?

Frustrated, he slammed his fist on the desk, rattling paper clips and files.

He forced himself to look at the pictures of the two girls who'd gone missing from Sunset Mesa the year before. Almost the same time of year.

Avery Portland and Melanie Hoit. Avery grew up with a single mother, worked at the ice cream shop and was voted most likely to succeed in her class. She was popular, on the dance team at school, and class president.

Melanie was a cheerleader, pretty and aspired to be a model. Some of her classmates described her as the girl everyone wanted to be. A few others commented that she was a snob.

But so far everyone they'd questioned had alibis.

And neither girl had been found. No body. No ransom calls.

Nothing.

The parents wanted closure just as the residents in Camden Crossing did.

He slumped down in the chair and glanced back at the photo of Tawny-Lynn. No wonder his parents and the other family members of the victims had turned on her.

She might be the only lead they had.

He understood people's anger and frustration.

But why would someone want to hurt her? Then she'd never be able to tell them who else had been there that day.

The answer hit him like a fist in the gut.

Someone didn't want her to remember because there had been foul play.

And if she could identify the culprit, she could put him or her in jail....

HE WATCHED THE house where Tawny-Lynn slept.

The images of the girls who'd died tormented him. He hadn't meant to kill them all. He loved them too much to do them harm.

But things had gotten out of hand. Then everything had gone wrong.

His gut churned with memories of the screams of those girls in the fire. That had been...terrible. He had nightmares to this day. He would never have wanted any of them to suffer like that.

His heart was racing as he remembered the panic that had seized him when the bus had exploded.

Ah, sweet Peyton. So easy to love.

And Ruth... He'd wanted her so badly back then.

Another few months and maybe Tawny-Lynn would have appealed to him, too. She did now.

So sexy and athletic and that soft, blond hair... She'd turned out to be pretty after all.

Too bad she might have to die.

Chapter Six

Tawny-Lynn couldn't go back to sleep. She didn't even want to go back to sleep, and relive the same old nightmare.

If only she could recall the face of the person who'd rescued her.

She climbed from bed, threw on a pair of jeans and a T-shirt and yanked her hair back into a ponytail. The mammoth job of cleaning the rest of the house awaited her.

But she needed coffee and food, and now that the kitchen was clean, she needed some groceries to get by on until she could make the necessary repairs to the ranch.

She jogged down the stairs, but the sound of her sister's voice called to her as if she was begging her to find her.

She grabbed her purse and cell phone, then remembered her car was in the shop. She'd seen the keys to her father's pickup somewhere. If it was still running, she'd take it into town.

She glanced around the living room, daunted by

the task she faced, then went back to the kitchen and remembered that she'd put the keys in the wicker basket with the bills that needed attention. Keys in hand, she jogged outside and found the truck parked beneath the makeshift carport her father had erected. The ancient truck was rusty and chugged and coughed as she tried to start it, as if it hadn't been cranked in ages. But her father had to have driven it to pick up his booze and the junk boxes he collected.

After three attempts, the battery finally charged to life, and she pulled from the carport. Remembering the intruder the night before, she scanned the property surrounding the ranch, but everything looked still and quiet.

Relieved, she barreled down the dirt drive and turned on the road to town. She passed the high school, pausing for a second to watch as the teenagers began to arrive. Students had gathered in the parking lot to hang out before going inside just as she and Ruth and Peyton used to do with the team. Softball season was almost over, and a sign out front congratulated the team for making it to the state finals. They were probably beginning playoffs now. Coach Wake was sure to be ecstatic.

She sped up, entered the town square and parked in front of the diner, desperate for coffee and breakfast. Thunderclouds darkened the sky, promising rain, and she pulled on her denim jacket and walked up the sidewalk to the diner. An old-fashioned hitching post and wagon wheel made the wooden structure look like a building from the past.

The delicious scent of bacon and coffee engulfed her when she entered, and her stomach growled. When had she eaten last?

She glanced around the room in search of an empty booth and suddenly felt tension charge the air. Voices quieted. Laughter died. A few whispers echoed through the diner.

Nerves climbed up her neck.

Suddenly Chaz appeared looking larger than life and so sexy that need spiraled through her.

"Good morning, Tawny-Lynn."

She wasn't so sure of that. "Maybe I should leave."

He shook his head. "No, sit down, have breakfast with me."

Did he know what he was doing? "I'm not sure that's a good idea."

He took her arm and ushered her into a booth to the left. "Well, I do. I'm sheriff. People had better take note."

Some emotion she couldn't define swelled inside her. She hadn't had anyone stand up for her in a long time.

She sank into the booth, exhausted already, and the day hadn't even begun. Chaz motioned for the waitress, and she appeared, a pencil jammed into her bouffant hairdo.

"Morning, Sheriff." She glanced down at Tawny-

Lynn, her penciled-in eyebrows knit together. "Hey, sugar. You new to town?"

Tawny-Lynn fiddled with the paper napkin as she read the woman's name tag. Her name was Hilda. "I used to live here. I'm Tawny-Lynn Boulder."

"Oh, right, hon, I heard you were coming home. So sorry about your daddy." Hilda set two coffee cups on the gingham tablecloth and filled them with coffee from the pot on her tray. "He used to come in for coffee every now and then."

When he was sober? Tawny-Lynn couldn't imagine.

But she relaxed at the woman's friendly smile.

"What'll you two have?"

"The breakfast special for me." Chaz grinned at Tawny-Lynn. "They make the best biscuits in town."

She noted the chalkboard. The special was three eggs, sausage and pancakes. If she ate all that, she'd be too full to get any work done.

"I'll take the country breakfast. Scrambled eggs with cheese."

"Sausage or bacon?"

"Sausage."

Hilda smiled again, then called their order in and headed to the next table.

"Did you sleep any last night?" Chaz asked.

She fiddled with her napkin. "A little. But I dreamed about the crash."

He was watching her, his interest piqued, but he didn't push. "You dream about it a lot?"

She nodded. "All the time."

"What happens in the dream?"

She tucked a strand of hair that had escaped the ponytail holder behind her ear. "I'm at the ball game. We win, everyone's excited, cheering. Then we run to the bus. Coach says we'll meet for pizza." Goose bumps skated up her arms.

"Then?"

"Then we're in the bus and everyone's talking and then the bus jerks…like someone hit us, and the driver loses control."

Chaz sucked in a sharp breath. "That fits with our theory."

"You believe someone caused the accident?"

"Yes, but we don't know if it was an accident, or if someone intentionally slammed into the bus."

Tawny-Lynn's gaze met his. She'd never heard the authority's theories or if they had any suspects. The sheriff had expected her to have the answers.

"Any leads on the driver of the vehicle who hit us?"

He shook his head. "A small paint sample was taken, but it got lost in the mess that came afterward."

A strained silence fell over them as Hilda brought their food. Chaz poured syrup on his pancakes and wolfed them down, while she made a breakfast sandwich with the eggs, biscuit and sausage. He was right. The biscuit melted in her mouth.

"Any more trouble last night?"

"No, thank goodness."

He sipped his coffee. "How'd you get into town?"

"Daddy's truck. It's old but it made it." She stirred sweetener into her coffee. "Guess I'll need to sell it, too." She shrugged. "Or maybe I'll just give it away. I doubt it's worth anything."

She felt someone beside them, then looked up at Coach Wake who'd stopped by the table. "Tawny-Lynn, I was sorry about your father. Are you here to stay and run the ranch?"

Her stomach clenched. She'd once loved softball more than anything in her life. The coach had been her and Peyton and Ruth's idol.

Now he was a reminder of the worst day of her life, and softball was a sport she couldn't stand to watch.

CHAZ FELT TAWNY-LYNN shutting down before his eyes. She'd been devouring her breakfast, but dropped the biscuit onto her plate and sipped her water.

"No, I'm not staying," she said, her voice warbling. "The ranch hasn't been a working ranch in a long time."

Coach Wake glanced at Chaz, then at Tawny-Lynn as if he were trying to dissect their relationship.

"Then you're going to sell it?" the coach asked.

Tawny-Lynn nodded. "Just as soon as I clean it up."

Coach Wake shifted as someone else passed by. "If you need help, Keith Plumbing can use the work. He did some repairs around my house. My wife thought he was reliable and did a good job."

Tawny-Lynn twisted her napkin into shreds. "Thanks for the reference."

"No problem."

Two teenage girls brushed by, then stopped to speak to the coach, both of them giggling. "Hey, Coach, thought you said you were laying off Donna's gravy."

He patted his stomach. "I need the calories to keep up with you girls. We're doing sprints this afternoon."

The girls groaned, then the redheaded one checked her watch. "We gotta go. We're going to miss first bell."

They rushed off, and Coach Wake rubbed his stomach. "Well, guess I'd better get to school. We have practice this afternoon. Did you know we made the play-offs?"

Tawny-Lynn took another sip of her coffee. "I saw the announcement on the marquis in front of the school on my way in to town. Congratulations."

The coach's smile broadened. "We've got a good team. But I haven't had a pitcher like you since you left. Stop by and watch the drills if you want. You could show the girls a thing or two."

"I don't think I'll have time, but thanks," she said. "I have my work cut out for me."

"Okay, but the offer still stands." He said goodbye to Chaz, then headed toward the door, but two women stopped him to chat on his way out. At least the coach had been friendly to Tawny-Lynn and hadn't treated her like a piranha like other people did.

If he remembered correctly, she'd been the star of the team and had won the game for them that last day.

His sister had adored the coach, too, just like all the girls had. And Coach Wake had cried like a baby at the funerals of the girls who hadn't survived the crash. He'd also been a leader in organizing search parties for Ruth and Peyton in the days following their disappearance.

"Are you okay?" Chaz asked.

A weary sigh escaped Tawny-Lynn. "Yes. But seeing him reminds me of…"

"Peyton and that day."

She nodded, her eyes glittering with tears as she looked up at him. His heart ached for her. Had anyone comforted her after the crash?

Did she have a boyfriend back in Austin?

He motioned to Hilda to bring the bill. It didn't

matter to him if she did have a boyfriend. She didn't want to be here in town, and he had a job to do.

He wouldn't let himself even think about a relationship with anyone until this case was solved and he gave his parents closure about Ruth.

TAWNY-LYNN NEEDED some air. The conversation with Coach Wake had stirred memories she tried hard to keep at bay.

Heck, everything about the town roused memories.

The diner was starting to clear as everyone paid their checks and left for work. A young man with blond hair, wearing jeans and a flannel shirt strode up to the table just as Chaz reached for the bill. Her fingers touched it at the same time and that annoying frisson of awareness sent a tingle through her.

"Chaz?"

"I've got it," he said with a look that warned her not to argue.

"Hey, Sheriff," the blond man said. "I got your message."

Chaz shook the guy's hand. "Yeah, Jimmy, this is Tawny-Lynn—the woman I told you about. She owns White Forks and needs new locks."

His eyes flashed a smile at her as he tipped his cowboy hat. He was handsome in a rugged, good-old-boy kind of way. "Hey, ma'am. I'm Jimmy James, I own the locksmith shop."

Tawny-Lynn shook his hand, annoyed that his hand didn't make her tingle.

No, only Chaz Camden's touch made her body quiver. The one man in town she could never be close to.

"I can get to those locks right away if you want."

"Thanks. I'm going to pick up some groceries, then head back out to the ranch."

He handed her his business card. "Give me a call when you get home, and I'll run out."

Home? White Forks was not her home anymore. But she didn't argue. She accepted his card, then sat stiffly as Chaz paid the bill. They walked outside to her father's truck together. Chaz leaned against it as she dug out her keys.

"I don't know if you should use Keith Plumbing to do those repairs." His mouth twitched into a frown. "There's something about the man that rubs me the wrong way."

"What?"

Chaz shrugged. "I don't know. But he was questioned after Ruth and Peyton went missing."

Tawny-Lynn jerked her head up. "You mean he was a suspect?"

"He was a person of interest," Chaz said. "He did some odd jobs for my parents, and he'd worked in Sunset Mesa around the same time the two girls went missing from that area."

Tawny-Lynn gritted her teeth. She didn't remember the man.

"How about the ranch? Did he do repairs there?"

Chaz shook his head. "Not according to your father."

"Was anyone else questioned as a suspect?"

"Barry Dothan," Chaz said. "Do you remember him? He was my age, but is mentally handicapped."

"I do remember seeing him around town. He was odd, used to hang out by the field and watch us practice," Tawny-Lynn said.

Chaz shrugged. "The sheriff found pictures of all the girls on the softball team and swim team plastered on his walls. But his mother claimed he was home the day of the crash."

"You think she'd lie to protect him?"

"That's hard to say. He has problems. She feels protective."

"I don't think he'd hurt anyone."

"Maybe not intentionally. But he could have gotten confused. Maybe he showed up and Peyton and Ruth were hurt and scared of him. He got mad. There were rocks out there. He could have used one on Ruth or Peyton."

And if her sister and Ruth had been injured, they might have been too weak to fight back.

"If he did hurt them, then why didn't you find their bodies? Surely, he wasn't smart enough to hide them somewhere."

"That's the reason the sheriff didn't think he

did it," Chaz said. "And the reason he was never arrested." Chaz reached for the truck door to open it for her. "I'm telling you so you'll watch out for him and Plumbing. If one of them had something to do with Ruth's and Peyton's disappearance, he might be worried about your memory returning."

Tawny-Lynn nodded. But she didn't intend to run like the person who'd written those bloody messages wanted.

If Plumbing or Barry Dothan knew something, she'd find out. She needed to know the truth in order to move on.

Chapter Seven

Tawny-Lynn left the diner, then walked across the street to the general store. She should have thought to buy groceries the night before, but she'd been overwhelmed by the dust and mess, and her only thought had been about cleaning.

She grabbed a cart as she entered, reminding herself that although she enjoyed cooking, she didn't have time for fancy meals and wouldn't be entertaining anyone. Most of her time would be spent cleaning out the house and working in the yard. She didn't plan to be at White Forks long. Maybe a week, no more.

Once she put the ranch on the market, she'd go back to Austin, and let the real-estate agent handle the rest.

She gathered coffee and sweetener, eggs, milk, cereal, bread, cheese, sandwich meat, added a few canned goods and soups, then decided to pick up ingredients to fix her favorite chili and nacho pie. Both would make enough to last her a couple of nights and were simple to prepare.

Relying on her favorite go-to recipes, she dropped in corn, black beans, tomatoes, tortillas and seasonings, then sour cream, avocados and limes to make guacamole.

The store was fairly empty, but as she rounded the corner to the produce section, she almost bumped into a middle-aged woman with an overflowing cart. A gray-haired man she assumed to be the woman's husband plucked a bag of oranges from a display table.

He scratched at his forehead when he spotted her. "Tawny-Lynn, is that you?"

Her hands tightened around the cart. "Sheriff Simmons?"

He chuckled and shook his head. "I'm not the sheriff anymore. Retired a couple of years ago. Chaz Camden took over."

"Yes, I know. I saw Chaz earlier."

Mrs. Simmons eyed her over her wire-rimmed glasses. "Sorry about your daddy, dear."

"Thanks." People probably judged her for not honoring him with a memorial service. Yet another reason for people to disapprove of her.

"What have you been doing with yourself?" Mr. Simmons asked.

"I started a landscaping business in Austin. I just came back to take care of the ranch."

He squeezed her arm. "I'm sorry we never found out what happened to Peyton and Ruth. That case will always haunt me."

Her throat thickened with emotions. "I know you did your best."

"Did your memory of that day ever return?" Mrs. Simmons asked, a hopeful note in her voice.

Tawny-Lynn shook her head. "No. I guess the doctor was wrong when he said the amnesia was temporary."

Guilt crawled through her, making her itch to run again. She gripped the cart and started away. "Well, it was nice to see you. I have to get back to the ranch."

"Nice to see you, too," the Simmonses said at once.

At least they'd been cordial to her, Tawny-Lynn thought, as she grabbed some fruit and headed to the checkout counter. The last time she'd talked to the sheriff he'd come out to the ranch when she'd been released from the hospital.

Everyone in town was hounding him to find Ruth and Peyton and get answers for the dead girls, and he'd interrogated her as if she'd caused the accident herself.

She paid for the groceries, then carried them outside and loaded them in her car. But as she pulled away, an eerie sense crept over her.

Was someone watching her?

She looked around, searching, but didn't see anyone suspicious. A mother and her baby strolling in the park, a family climbing into their SUV, an elderly man walking into the hardware store leaning on a horsehead cane.

She was just being paranoid.

Still, she stayed alert as she drove through town, then found herself driving the opposite direction from home, out on Dirt Dauber Road, a road named after the mud daubers that had built nests in the cylinder of a small plane, causing it to crash. Oddly, that crash had occurred only a mile from where the school bus had collided into the boulder below the ridge.

Perspiration beaded on her neck as she parked, but she took a deep breath to calm herself. She had visited this site twice during the year after the accident, each time hoping it would trigger her memory.

Both times she'd had such panic attacks that she'd collapsed.

She was not going to do that today. She had to hold it together.

Determined, she walked over to the edge of the ridge. The guardrail had not only been repaired, but a sturdier metal one that was at least four inches higher had replaced it. Still the distance to the bottom of the ravine was daunting.

The wind stirred the leaves in the trees, their rustling sound mingling with the rumble of the brewing storm. The skies had darkened again, blotting out the sun.

She stared at the boulder below, an image of the bus teetering over the edge flashing into her mind. Was that a memory or simply a figment of her imagination due to the pictures and descriptions she'd seen?

A scream echoed in her head and she closed her eyes for a moment, launching back in time.

The ball game, the victory, they were going to get pizza, Ruth and Peyton whispering about some guy...then the jolt.

Had she looked back to see what had hit them?

No...no time. The bus lurched forward, was losing control. Screams, blood, glass shattering, metal scraping... then a loud crunch. She was falling, falling, struggling to grab hold of something to keep from going through the glass...

Then pain and she couldn't move, and...darkness. Then hands touching her, a low voice whispering she would be all right. Fresh air hit her, and she gulped, her chest aching as she drew in a breath. But when she opened her eyes the face was dark. Blank. As if wearing a mask.

No, not a mask. As if there was no face...

SHE OPENED HER eyes, her breathing coming in erratic pants. Why couldn't she see the face?

Frustrated, she kicked at a rock and watched it tumble down the dirt into the ravine.

Suddenly that eerie feeling swept over her again, and she felt someone behind her. Watching her.

She must be paranoid, she reminded herself.

But when she glanced over her shoulder, a shadow moved. Trees rustled. Leaves crunched.

It wasn't her imagination this time. A man was standing in the shadows, half hidden by the thick trees.

Not just any man—Barry Dothan.

And he was taking pictures of her from his hiding spot in the woods.

CHAZ DROVE TO Sunset Mesa and parked at the sheriff's office. He'd phoned ahead and Amanda Blair, the new sheriff of Sunset Mesa, had agreed to meet him.

He smelled coffee brewing as he entered and found a young woman in her twenties with amber hair pulled back into a ponytail pouring a mug at the scarred counter across from the front desk. She was petite but athletic looking, and as she turned, he noticed a steely glint in her eyes.

She might be compact, but her attitude screamed that she was tough and could handle the job.

He tipped his hat. "I'm here to meet the sheriff."

She offered him a smile. "I'm the sheriff, Amanda Blair." She extended her hand, and he shook it. "And don't even start with how young I look. My father was a Texas Ranger. I started solving crimes when I was in diapers."

He chuckled. "Sheriff Chaz Camden. Thanks for agreeing to meet me. And I wasn't going to comment on your age."

Her wry look indicated she knew he was lying. "Right." She gestured toward the coffee, and he nodded, then waited while she poured him a mug. Then she led him to a desk in an adjoining office.

"What can I do for you, Chaz?"

He liked her directness and dropped into a wooden chair across from her desk. "I don't know if your former sheriff shared information about our cold case with you."

She drummed her nails on the desk. "He didn't, but then again, Lager was having memory problems." She sighed. "The mayor gave him a lot of leeway, but finally they had to ask him to step down."

"I'm sorry." He laid the file he'd brought with him on the desk. "A few years ago, two girls went missing from Sunset Mesa. That same year, a bus carrying the local softball team crashed in Camden Crossing and took three girls' lives. One survived, but two others—Peyton Boulder and my sister, Ruth—disappeared. We still don't know what happened to them."

"I read about the cases," Sheriff Blair said. "I made it a point to familiarize myself with all the old files when I took office. Besides, I grew up around here and remembered the town's devastation when the girls went missing." She pulled a file from the drawer in the desk, opened it and placed it so he could read the contents.

"This is what I have so far on the missing girls from our area."

"Avery Portland was fifteen, popular, a cheer-leader. Parents dropped her off for a school dance. According to her boyfriend, she was acting funny all night, picked a fight and she went outside. He went after her, but she was gone."

"Boyfriend's story check out?"

Sheriff Blair shrugged. "He appeared to be dev-astated. His buddies all gave him an alibi, too."

"How about girl two?"

"Melanie Hoit, sixteen. On the dance team at school. Disappeared from the mall in Amarillo where she was supposed to meet her girlfriends on a Saturday night. Security cameras turned up nothing. According to parents, everyone loved her."

"Were either of the girls ever in trouble?"

She shook her head. "According to the families, no. Neither had any kind of arrest record. Both ex-celled in school. No problems with authority, al-though Avery's father had abandoned the family eight months before, and her friends said she was angry and had been to see the counselor about the divorce."

"Were she and Melanie friends?"

She nodded. "Since fifth grade."

Like Ruth and Peyton, except they'd disappeared without a trace.

"No ransom calls. No phone calls from the girls."

Sheriff Blair rubbed her hand over her forehead. "No leads."

Chaz spread the notes from the Camden case on the desk. "Sounds similar to our missing girls."

"Except for the bus crash," Sheriff Blair pointed out. "Avery and Melanie disappeared at different times."

Chaz chewed the inside of his cheek. "True. One theory is that the kidnapper was obsessed with one of them. But when the crash occurred, he had to take both."

Sheriff Blair narrowed her eyes. "But he left that other girl, Peyton's sister."

"Yes, Tawny-Lynn Boulder," Chaz said, his chest clenching. "That's true, but she had a broken leg and was unconscious."

"So how did he make two girls go with him? Were there signs of a struggle?"

Chaz grimaced. "It was hard to sort out what happened." He slid a photo of the crash site and tapped it. "There were skid marks from the bus and another vehicle, although the sheriff and crime team never tracked down the vehicle."

"What about blood from a fight? If the girls struggled with the abductor, there might have been evidence."

"The scene was a mess," Chaz said. "Blood and glass were on the rocks, but the fire destroyed most evidence. And it rained that day so the rain washed away the rest."

"I suppose if the kidnapper had a gun he could have forced the girls to go with him. But if Tawny-Lynn was injured, how did her sister and yours escape the bus unharmed?"

Chaz's chest tightened. "They could have been hurt, which would have made it harder for them to fight back," he said. "No one knows."

"What about the girl who survived? It says in the file that she might have witnessed the abduction."

Chaz nodded. "She sustained a head injury, had amnesia and can't remember details of that day."

Still, someone wanted her dead. Which confirmed in his mind that she had seen foul play.

Chaz removed three other photos and showed them to her. "These three young women have also gone missing during the past five years from various counties in Texas."

"You think they're connected?"

"I'm not sure, but maybe. The M.O. is the same. The victims are around the same age. All went missing in the spring, and vanished without a trace."

"Spring?" Sheriff Blair scowled. "The time of year might be significant."

Chaz nodded. What worried him most was that they had no leads. "If the same perpetrator kidnapped all these girls, that means another girl might go missing any day now."

Tawny-Lynn froze, her nerves sizzling with tension.

Barry Dothan had seemed harmless when she'd known him years ago. He was almost childlike in his speech patterns, and walked and behaved like an oversize kid. He'd gained weight and had a pudgy look about him now, his jowls were sagging, his dirty blond hair wiry and choppy as if he'd cut it himself.

But he was hiding and taking pictures of her. And the police had found pictures of Peyton and Ruth as well as other teenagers on the bulletin board in his room.

She shivered.

Was he going to add hers to that wall?

She slowly moved toward the woods, determined to talk to him. But panic flashed in his eyes when he saw her, and he started to run.

"Wait," Tawny-Lynn called.

He planted one hand on a tree, his eyes darting in all directions. She glanced around for a car, then noticed a bicycle tucked against a copse of trees.

"Barry?"

"I...didn't do anything wrong."

Tawny-Lynn forced her expression to remain calm. "I just want to talk to you."

"I didn't do anything," he mumbled again. "I just like to take pictures."

"It's all right," she said. "But why are you here?"

He shook his head from side to side, back and

forth in a frantic motion, his eyes widening in a crazed expression. "I didn't do anything!"

Then he jumped on his bike and raced back through the woods, weaving and swaying as if she'd frightened him.

Her heart raced as she jumped in the truck and fired up the engine. Barry might have been obsessed with her sister or Ruth, but would he have hurt them?

Maybe he'd tried to help them that day, but one of them had fought him and things had gone ugly....

But Chaz was right. He didn't have the intellect or enough emotional control to have hidden a body or kept quiet all these years.

Still, the way he protested so vehemently made her wonder if he knew something that he hadn't told. Maybe he'd been here that day and seen something?

The truck chugged around the winding road, her mind trying to picture the blank face in her memory. Could it have been Barry who'd pulled her from the fire?

She turned down the drive to White Forks, angry that her mind refused to give her the answers she needed.

The answer everyone in town needed, especially the Camdens and the parents of the deceased girls.

She threw the truck into Park, retrieved two of the grocery bags and started toward the porch steps. But she froze at the bottom, her breath catching.

A dead animal, maybe a deer, had been slaughtered and left on the porch. A bloody trail was smeared on the steps.

And another message had been written in blood on the door.

Leave, or this will be you next.

Chapter Eight

Chaz had just left Sunset Mesa when his phone rang. His stomach knotted when he saw Tawny-Lynn's number on the screen.

"Hello."

"Chaz, I hate to bother you—"

"What's wrong?"

"Someone left a slaughtered deer on my front porch with another message."

Chaz silently released a string of expletives. "Don't touch anything and don't go inside."

"I haven't. I'm sitting in the truck."

"Good. I'll be there as soon as I can." He jogged outside, jumped in his squad car, flipped on the siren and sped away from Sunset Mesa, his phone glued to his ear. "Did you see anyone when you pulled up?"

"No," Tawny-Lynn said.

"Has Jimmy been there to redo the locks?"

"Not yet. I'm expecting him any minute."

"Okay, just keep your eyes peeled. If you see

anyone, get out of there. Don't try to confront them on your own."

"Don't worry. I don't have a death wish," she said.

But someone else had one for her. He turned onto the main highway leading back to Camden Crossing. "I just came from talking to the sheriff in Sunset Mesa about the two girls that went missing from there the year before Ruth and Peyton did."

"Didn't Sheriff Simmons already cover that?"

"Yeah, but it turns out the sheriff in Sunset Mesa was suffering from dementia. I thought fresh eyes might see something they missed back then."

"Any luck?"

"No. But I'm not giving up." A thick silence fell between them. "Tawny-Lynn, are you okay?"

"Yes," she said, although she didn't sound okay.

How could she be with threats being made against her? "Did something else happen?"

A weary sigh echoed back. "I stopped by the site of the bus crash."

A heartbeat passed. He didn't know what to say. Everyone had pushed her to remember, yet that day had been traumatic and painful for her. "And?"

"I remember someone slamming into the bus and us careening over the side of the ridge," she said. "But I didn't see who hit us. And...then I remember being unconscious and waking up and someone was pulling me from the wreckage. Smoke was billowing around me, and the heat…it was so hot and I was scared."

Chaz's heart was pounding, but he didn't push. He simply waited to see if she would elaborate.

"But that's it," she whispered. "The face is… blank."

He slowed as he rounded a curve, then passed the high school.

"Maybe you didn't actually see the face," he suggested.

"I…don't know." Her voice cracked. "I feel like I did, but there's something in my way, blocking out the image."

"You were injured," Chaz said softly. It was about time someone cut her some slack.

Another tense minute passed, while he veered down the driveway to the ranch.

She cleared her throat. "There's something else."

He scrubbed a hand through his hair as the farmhouse slipped into view. "What?"

"Today when I was at the site. I felt like someone was watching me, and when I looked over my shoulder, Barry Dothan was there, hiding in the woods, taking pictures of me."

Fear slammed into Chaz. "Did he hurt you?"

"No," Tawny-Lynn said. "But it was spooky. I tried to talk to him, but he kept shouting that he hadn't done anything wrong."

"Did he say what he meant by that?"

"No. But why would he go back there if he wasn't there when the accident happened?"

"Good question. I'll have a talk with him and his mother. Maybe he did something to the girls accidentally. If not, maybe he knows something."

Chaz raced up beside the truck and parked, then jumped out, his gun drawn. Tawny-Lynn opened the truck door and climbed down, her face pale.

He took one look at the bloody deer carcass and message on her porch and fury railed inside him.

"I have to do something to stop this," she whispered.

"It's not your fault," Chaz said between gritted teeth.

Then he did what he'd wanted to do when he saw the very first message. He pulled her up against him and wrapped his arms around her.

TAWNY-LYNN LEANED into Chaz, her body trembling. Ever since that awful accident, she'd felt alone.

Persecuted, confused, terrified and guilt-ridden.

She'd learned to deal with it and to stand on her own, but for just a moment, she allowed herself the comfort of Chaz's arms.

He stroked her back, rubbing slow circles between her shoulder blades. "You don't deserve this, Tawny-Lynn, and I'm going to make sure whoever did this doesn't hurt you."

Tension slowly seeped from her tightly wound muscles. She felt the warmth of his arms encircling her, the soft rise and fall of his chest against her cheek, the whisper of his breath against her ear.

Finally she raised her gaze to his. "I'm sorry, Chaz. I guess that dead animal shook me up more than I thought."

His eyes darkened with concern and other emotions that made her want to reach up and touch his cheek.

Kiss his lips.

Foolish.

A muscle ticked in his jaw. "I promise you I'll put a stop to this cruelty."

She pulled away and struggled for bravado. "Whoever did it probably just wants to scare me off."

"Maybe so. But I won't tolerate this kind of crap while I'm in office. When I find the bastard who did it, he'll pay."

She folded her arms, missing his contact already. The sound of an engine rumbled, and a black pickup rolled up.

"There's Jimmy now." Chaz flicked a hand up to greet the locksmith as he emerged from his truck. "We have a problem here," he said, indicating the carcass on the front porch. "Let me check the house out first, then you can get to work."

Chaz gestured to Tawny-Lynn. "Stay here with her until I return." Then he raced up the steps to the house.

Tawny-Lynn hissed a breath, praying the person who'd threatened her wasn't inside.

Jimmy shuffled back and forth. "Sorry you're having trouble, ma'am."

Tawny-Lynn forced a polite smile. Jimmy was probably in his thirties and wore jeans and a khaki shirt with the name *James's Locks* embroidered on the pocket. His smile was flirty like it had been at the diner although a devilish gleam lit his eyes.

But Chaz must trust him or he wouldn't have called him.

"You didn't grow up in Camden Crossing, did you?" she asked.

"No, ma'am," Jimmy said. "I came from Sunset Mesa. But I moved here a couple years ago."

Chaz returned to the doorway and waved that the house was safe. "I'll clean up this mess, Jimmy, and you can start with the locks."

Jimmy nodded, grabbed a kit from his car and headed up to the porch. "You want a security system?"

Tawny-Lynn frowned and shook her head. "I don't think installing a security system is worth the investment."

Chaz didn't look convinced. "Put dead bolts on all the doors and check the window locks. Then install a hidden camera and aim it at this porch. If this guy shows up again, we'll nail him."

Tawny-Lynn waited until Chaz hauled the bloody deer carcass off the porch. He carried it into the woods, and she retrieved the groceries, sidestepping the blood on the porch floor as she carried them inside.

She quickly sorted and stored the items, glad she'd cleaned the pantry of the outdated canned and boxed goods. Chaz came in for more bleach and a bucket of water and sponge.

Jimmy started in the kitchen with the back door, giving Chaz time to clean the front porch. She brewed a pot of coffee and left it for the men, then started to clean the den.

But the memory of Barry Dothan at the crash site made her rethink her plan. Instead of starting downstairs, she'd start in Peyton's room.

She and Ruth had been whispering about boys those last few weeks, sharing secrets and giggling and talking in hushed voices. Every time she'd tried to join the conversation, her sister had shut her out.

What if her boyfriend knew something?

Maybe there was some clue in Peyton's room as to the secret they'd been sharing.

CHAZ HAD PHOTOGRAPHED the deer and bloody message before he hauled the carcass into the woods. Then he searched for fingerprints on the door, but other than the blood, the door had been wiped clean. There were also no footprints in the blood so the perpetrator had sidestepped the bloody trail he'd left on the steps.

Someone knew what he was doing and was covering his tracks.

But who?

There were a dozen or so people who didn't want Tawny-Lynn here.

Because they didn't want her to remember what happened that day? To remember the face she said was blank?

Because he or she had done something to Ruth and Peyton?

That thought made his gut churn, and he punched the number for the crime lab and asked to speak to Lieutenant Willis Ludlow, the CSI chief he'd met at a police seminar.

"What can I do for you?" Lieutenant Ludlow asked.

Chaz quickly explained the circumstances. "My deputy couriered over some blood samples I took at the crime scene."

"Yeah, hang on a minute, and I'll pull the results."

Paper rustled, then a tapping sound followed, and he realized Ludlow was on his computer. Seconds later, he returned. "Okay, the blood sample on the mirror came from an animal. It was dried and had been there a couple of days."

Two days—the same day Tawny-Lynn's father had died. "Deer blood?"

"No, a rabbit."

"And the blood on the wall?"

"That one was from a deer. Maybe your guy is a hunter."

"Possibly." Or anyone with enough imagination to kill a deer and use its blood to frighten Tawny-Lynn.

His mind ticked away possibilities. It had to be someone fairly strong to have dragged the deer up onto the porch. Someone who didn't have a weak stomach.

Most likely a man.

"How about the prints?"

"The only ones we found were Boulder's and his daughter's."

Chaz was frustrated but not surprised.

"Sorry, I know that's not much help."

"This perp is covering his tracks," Chaz said. "But I'll catch him sooner or later." He just hoped it was before the creep tried to make good on his threats and hurt Tawny-Lynn.

His conversation with his father echoed in his head, and he went to tell Tawny-Lynn that he was leaving.

He needed to have a talk with his old man.

But there was no reason his father wouldn't want Tawny-Lynn to remember. In fact, he'd driven the theory that she'd been hiding something and demanded she stop faking the amnesia.

But his father didn't want her here, and he had a hunting rifle. Deer hunting was his sport.

Then he'd talk to Barry Dothan about those pictures and see if he was stalking Tawny-Lynn.

TAWNY-LYNN SHIVERED as she stepped into her sister's old room. It was as if she'd walked back in time.

Peyton had always been his favorite because she was more of a girly-girl, and her room reflected her personality.

Though she and her father had argued those last few months. Mostly about the length of Peyton's skirts, her makeup and boyfriends. Peyton had been hormonal, determined to date when their father told her no, and had snuck out several times late at night.

Her father had also found her slipping alcohol from the house.

Twice, she'd come in so drunk she could barely walk, and Tawny-Lynn had covered for her. She and her sister had argued the next day, and Tawny-Lynn had begged her sister to stop acting out.

Peyton had yelled that she was almost eighteen, that she was in love, and that she'd do whatever she pleased.

A couple of weeks later, she'd run in crying one night, and when Tawny-Lynn asked what was wrong, Peyton refused to talk.

She'd figured it was boyfriend trouble, but then she'd heard Peyton and Ruth arguing over the phone later, and thought the two of them had had a falling out. But Peyton had never shared what had upset her or what happened between her and Ruth.

She slid into the desk chair in the corner and searched the drawers, finding assorted junk—spiral notebooks with old algebra problems, a science notebook, movie ticket stubs, old hair bows, ribbons and report cards. Peyton had been an average student, but popular because of her good looks.

She checked the other drawers and found a few photographs of her sister and Ruth. The two of them at pep rallies, Peyton playing midfield, Peyton in her homecoming dress, Ruth in hers on the homecoming court.

Her finger brushed the edge of something, and she discovered another photo jammed between two school albums.

Her heart squeezed as she stared at the picture. It was Peyton, her and their mother. Peyton had probably been two and she was an infant. Her mother was smiling as she cradled her in her arms.

Tawny-Lynn wiped at a tear and placed the photo in her pocket to keep. If her mother had lived, how would their lives been different? Would her father have stayed away from the bottle?

Satisfied the desk held no clues, she checked the nightstand by the bed. Her sister had kept a diary, but Tawny-Lynn searched for it after Peyton disappeared and never found it. It could have been in her gym bag in the bus and burned in the fire.

Another lead lost.

In the drawer beneath an old compact and brush, she found a box of condoms. She opened the box of twelve and noted they were half gone. Peyton had always had boyfriends, but she hadn't known her sister was sexually active.

Who had she been sleeping with?

Hoping to find some clue about the mysterious boyfriend or the missing diary, she rummaged through the closet, searching the shoeboxes on the floor but found nothing but sneakers, sandals, flip-flops and a pair of black dress shoes.

Deciding it was time to throw out her sister's clothes—she could donate them to the church along with her father's belongings—she gathered several garbage bags and began pulling sweaters, shirts and jeans off the shelves and rack and dumping them inside.

She spotted Peyton's letter jacket and pulled it off the hanger, but a folded scrap of paper fell from the pocket. She opened the note and read it.

Dear Peyton,
Please don't leave me. I love you, and you said
you loved me. Call me tonight.
Love & Kisses,
J.J.

Tawny-Lynn struggled to remember J.J.'s last name. The class yearbooks were in the desk drawer, so she grabbed the latest one and searched the names and photos from the senior class.

J.J. McMullen.

Yes, Peyton had been dating him around Christmastime.

Did he still live around town?

She used her smart phone to look up his number and found a James McMullen living right outside town. She punched his number but a woman answered. "Hello?"

Tawny-Lynn wiped dust from her jeans. "I'm looking for James McMullen."

"He's at work. Who is this?"

A baby's cry echoed somewhere in the background.

"Where does he work?"

"At the meat market in town. Now who is this?"

Tawny-Lynn didn't reply. She hung up, trying to picture the dark-haired boy who Peyton had once dated butchering meat all day, but the image didn't fit.

But his father had owned the place so he must have gone to work with him.

She finished cleaning out the closet, then stripped the dusty bedcovers and stuffed them in another bag. The notebooks and papers went into the trash. When she finished, she dragged the bags downstairs.

"I'm finished down here," Jimmy said. "I'll check the windows upstairs."

"Thanks."

She hauled the bags of clothes outside, tossed them into the pickup truck and headed to the church. She dropped the bags with the secretary, thinking the woman looked familiar, but she didn't take the time to introduce herself.

Ten minutes later, she parked in front of the meat market and went inside. Glass cases held dozens of cuts of beef, pork and chicken while shelves to the side were filled with homegrown vegetables, sauces and spices.

An older man with a receding hairline stood behind the counter, his apron stained.

"Mr. McMullen?" Tawny-Lynn asked.

His reading glasses wobbled as he peered over the counter at her. "What can I do for you, young lady?"

"I'd like to talk to your son, J.J."

The man frowned, but yelled his son's name. A second later, J.J. appeared, looking more like his father than she remembered. Maybe it was the receding hairline or the nose that was slightly crooked. The bloody apron didn't help.

"Tawny-Lynn?" J.J. said, his eyes widening in recognition.

She nodded, then removed the note and gestured for him to take it. He rounded the counter and leaned against the potato bin as he read it.

"You were the last guy I remember dating Peyton before she disappeared."

His sharp gaze jerked toward her. "You think I had something to do with that?"

"No," Tawny-Lynn said, although the anger in his tone made her wonder. Had he been questioned seven years ago?

"In the note, you were asking her not to leave you. What happened?"

He cut his eyes toward his father, then shoved the note back in her hands. "She dumped me, that's what happened. She found someone else."

"Did she say who it was?"

He shook his head, his anger palpable. "No, but I got the impression it was an older man. She kept saying that it was complicated, but that he was sophisticated and he'd take care of her. That one day they'd get married." His gaze met hers. "Hell, when she went missing, I thought maybe she ran off with him."

Tawny-Lynn had heard that rumor. But the sheriff had found no evidence to substantiate the theory.

It was complicated.

What if her sister had been seeing an older man, maybe a *married* man? If she told J.J. her intentions of marrying, maybe Peyton had pressured him to leave his wife.

Would he have hurt her sister to keep their affair quiet?

Chapter Nine

Chaz should have been relieved that the messages had been written in animal blood instead of human blood, but the fact that someone had threatened an innocent woman in his town infuriated him.

He parked in front of the bank and strode in, then headed straight to his father's office, but the secretary stopped him on the way.

"He's not here. He went home to have lunch with your mother."

That was a surprise. But it probably meant that he'd found some discrepancy in their finances and wanted to interrogate his mother. Gerome Camden was a control freak who had made a fortune because he obsessed over every penny, kept his wife on a tight budget and didn't allow frivolities.

Except where Ruth had been concerned. He'd doted on her and spoiled her rotten.

Chaz drove to his parents' house, tossing a quick wave to the gardener trimming the shrubs, then buzzed the doorbell. He didn't wait for the maid to answer, but had only buzzed to alert them he was on his way.

His boots clicked on the polished-marble floor in the entryway as he crossed to the dining room. His mother looked up with a smile, her china teacup halfway to her mouth. "Chaz, this is a surprise." She started to rise. "I'll get Harriet to bring you a plate."

"No thanks, Mom, I'm not here to eat." He crossed the room and gave her a quick kiss on the cheek.

"Of course you'll eat with us," his father said in a tone that brooked no argument.

Chaz rounded on him. He hated to broach this subject in front of his mother, but if anyone could calm his father—and keep him from doing something stupid to Tawny-Lynn—she could. Where Gerome Camden ruled the finances, Beverly Camden ruled the house and had impeccable manners and morals.

"What's going on?" his mother asked.

Chaz set the file he'd brought with him on the table in front of his father. "When Dad heard Tawny-Lynn Boulder was coming back to town, he paid me a visit and ordered me to run her out of town."

"What?" His mother fanned her face. "Gerome, you didn't."

Guilt streaked his father's face. "We suffered

enough seven years ago because of that girl. I didn't want her stirring up old hurts."

"You act as if she caused the bus accident," his mother chided. "She lost her sister, too, and she spent a week in the hospital."

"That's right." Chaz opened the folder and spread out the photos of the bloody messages. "When she arrived, she found this on the mirror in her room. That night someone ran her off the road into a ditch." He tapped the photo of the bathroom wall. "Then someone left this."

"Is that blood?" his mother asked.

Chaz nodded. "Rabbit blood on the mirror. Deer blood on the wall." He showed them the picture of the bloody deer carcass. "When she got home from the grocery store today, this was waiting for her."

His mother made a choked sound and grabbed her water, but his father simply glared at him. "I told you no one wanted her here."

"Did you do this, Dad? Or did you hire someone to?"

His father slammed both hands on the table, jarring the silverware. "How dare you accuse me of such a thing. Just look how you've upset your mother."

Chaz planted his fists on his hips. "I'm not going anywhere until you answer my question."

"Chaz, you can't really believe—"

"Mother, please, let him answer." Chaz turned

to his father. "I know that you want Tawny-Lynn gone. Did you set this up to scare her off?"

"Of course not." His father shoved the pictures back into Chaz's hands. "Now take these offensive things and get them out of here."

Chaz gripped the folder. "I hope you're being honest, Dad. Because if I find out you had anything to do with this, I'll be back."

He mumbled an apology to his mother, then strode toward the door. Behind him, he heard ice clinking in a glass as his father fixed himself a scotch.

TAWNY-LYNN TRIED to remember the names of Peyton's other friends.

The softball team had been Tawny-Lynn's core group, and she'd been devastated at the deaths of her fellow teammates.

But Peyton had run in several groups. She'd chaired the prom committee her junior year, had worked on the class yearbook and joined the dance team during football season.

Cindy Miller, the cheerleading captain, had invited Peyton to a sleepover a few weeks before the accident. Desperate, Tawny-Lynn looked up the girls' name online and found her home address, so she called the number.

"Mrs. Miller speaking."

"Can I speak to Cindy please?"

"Cindy's not here. She's at her house. Who is this?"

Tawny-Lynn hesitated over revealing her name. "I'm calling from the high school reunion committee. We had a worm in the system that trashed our files, and we lost married names and current contact information."

"Oh, well, Cindy wouldn't miss a high school reunion for anything. She married Donny Parker from the class two years ahead of her. They live outside Camden Crossing in one of the homes on the lake. Donny developed the property himself."

So they were probably rolling in money. "That's wonderful. Can I have her phone number and address? And oh, if she works, I'd like that number, too."

She scribbled down the numbers as Cindy's mother read them off.

"Cindy doesn't work. She stays home with the twins."

Tawny-Lynn rolled her eyes. She probably had a nanny and spent her days at the tennis courts.

"Thanks. I'll give her a call." She disconnected, then wheeled the truck toward the lake. The storm clouds brewing all day looked darker as she passed farmland that would soon be rich with crops. White Forks once had a nice garden but her father had let it dry up along ago.

A few wildflowers had sprouted along the entrance to the lake community, the sign swaying in the wind. She followed the road through the wooded lots, noting that it was new and most of them weren't developed yet. No doubt expensive homes would be popping up, drawing newcomers to Camden Crossing.

Those lots would need landscaping. Designs rose to her mind, but she squashed the thought. No one in Camden Crossing would likely hire her to design their properties. No use in even going there.

She passed an estate lot where the house sat back in the woods and realized it was the address she was looking for. A personalized sign with the name Parker on it dangled from the mailbox, and as she veered down the driveway tall trees surrounded her, offering privacy and shade from the relentless Texas sun.

The stucco-and-stone house looked like a lodge nestled in the woods, and a BMW was parked in the garage. Beside the house, a boat ramp held a customized pontoon. Tawny-Lynn walked up the cobblestone steps leading to the front door and rang the doorbell. Seconds later, a commotion sounded inside with the sound of children squealing.

When the door opened, a pair of redheaded little boys stared up at her, their faces streaked in something that looked suspiciously like mud but smelled like chocolate pudding. She guessed them to be about four years old.

"Boys, I told you not to open the door!"

Tawny-Lynn swallowed her surprise when Cindy appeared. Maybe it was baby weight, but she'd gained at least thirty pounds.

"Tawny-Lynn?" Cindy said in a croaked whisper.

"Hi, Cindy. I wasn't sure you'd remember me."

"How could I forget?" The annoyance at the boys morphed into a wary look. Cindy did not look happy to see her.

"Mind if I come in and talk to you for a minute?"

"I can't imagine what about," Cindy said warily.

Bored, the boys took off running up the winding staircase behind them, screaming as they went.

"Please," she said. "I'm only back for a few days to get my father's ranch ready to sell."

Cindy bit her lower lip, shifting from one foot to the other as if struggling with her thoughts. Finally she motioned for her to come in.

"You have a gorgeous place," Tawny-Lynn said. "Your mother said you married Donny Parker, that he built these houses."

Nerves flashed in Cindy's eyes. "You talked to my mother?"

"I was just trying to remember some of Peyton's old friends."

Cindy's brown eyes widened. "Why? Have you heard from your sister?"

Tawny-Lynn fought the temptation to fidget as she took a seat on a leather sofa in the giant-size den. The view of the lake was magnificent, reminiscent of a postcard.

Cindy seemed to have everything in life. So why did she seem so anxious?

"No. Have you?"

Cindy raked kids' toys off the couch. "No, of course not. I just thought…maybe you found out what happened to her and Ruth."

"That's why I'm asking questions," Tawny-Lynn said. "I talked to J.J. McMullen earlier and he said that Peyton broke up with him for an older guy. He hinted that he thought the man might have been married. Did she ever mention anything to you about a man she was seeing?"

The sound of the children tearing down the stairs echoed in the cavernous house, and Cindy jumped up. "No, I don't remember that. Now I really need to take care of the boys. It's time for their karate lesson."

Tawny-Lynn stood, wondering if the boys really had a lesson, or if Cindy just wanted to get rid of her.

Because Cindy ushered her out the door and practically slammed it in her face.

Irritated, Tawny-Lynn drove down the long drive, then parked off to the side in a vacant lot and watched as seconds later, Cindy flew past.

What in the world was she in such a hurry for? The boys' lesson, or had her questions upset Cindy? Did she know whom Peyton had been seeing?

And if so, why hadn't she told her or the police?

CHAZ WAS STILL stewing with anger as he left his father's. Maybe he'd jumped the gun in his accusations.

His father was a businessman, a well-respected

member of the town, a man who used his money and connections to run the show.

But he'd never been violent or used physical force to get what he wanted. He'd never had to.

And smearing blood on a wall was not his style.

He drove to Barry Dothan's house, contemplating his approach. He'd found pictures of teenagers in the sheriff's file from the original investigation.

But Barry's mother had given him an alibi.

Still, he didn't like the fact that he'd been watching Tawny-Lynn.

He pulled over at the trailer park, noting the weed-choked yards dividing the mobile homes. Children's toys were scattered around, a mutt was tied to the porch that had been added on to the second trailer, then he spotted Barry's bike.

Chaz walked up to the trailer and knocked, remembering the stories he'd heard about the family. When she was younger, Mrs. Dothan had been a stripper and that's where she'd met Barry's father. He was now serving time in prison for selling cocaine.

Complications during childbirth had caused Barry's brain damage.

He knocked again and heard shuffling inside. The door screeched open and Mrs. Dothan stood looking at him with blurry eyes as if she'd been drinking. She wore a ratty housecoat that she tugged around her, then lit a cigarette, inhaled and blew out smoke.

"What do you want, Sheriff?"

"To talk to you and Barry." Chaz didn't wait on an invitation. He shouldered his way past her into the tiny den, which was riddled with dirty laundry and reeked of smoke and alcohol.

She dropped into a recliner that had seen better days, focusing on her cigarette.

"Is Barry here?"

"What you want him for? He do something?"

"I don't know," Chaz said. "Did he?"

She shrugged. "He's a good boy. Not bright, but he ain't bad."

Chaz walked toward the bedrooms. "Barry?"

"He ain't here," she said in a smoker's voice. "Now tell me what you want with him."

"I heard he was out at the site of the bus crash." He didn't have to elaborate. Everyone in town knew the place, the date, the time. It had been embedded in their memories forever. Some even used it as a reference point—before the bus crash, after the bus crash.

She shrugged. "He likes to ride his bike all over."

"He likes to take pictures, too. I saw the ones the sheriff confiscated seven years ago."

Her right eye twitched. "They were pictures of the girls at school, after softball practice, at the swim meet," she said. "Not like they were naked pictures."

Chaz arched a brow. "Does he have pictures of naked girls?"

She took another drag of her cigarette. "He may not be bright, but he's a guy," she said.

"Are they of real girls or are you talking magazines?"

"Those magazines. I don't know where he gets 'em but he keeps them under his bed. He doesn't know I found 'em."

Chaz shifted, curious. "Do you mind if I take a look in your son's room?"

She flicked ashes into a misshapen ashtray that Barry had obviously made out of clay. "Not if you're trying to pin something on him. I told the sheriff years ago Barry was with me the day of that crash. He didn't have nothing to do with it."

"I didn't say he did, but earlier he was taking photographs of Tawny-Lynn Boulder. It spooked her."

"Barry's not dangerous. Why's she acting like that?"

"Because someone left bloody threats on her doorstep and in her house."

Her eye twitched again, and she reached for a half-empty vodka bottle on the table. "He didn't leave any threats."

Chaz gestured to the bedroom with the posters of the high school swim and soccer teams. "If he's innocent, then it won't hurt for me to take a look." This time he didn't wait for her response.

He ducked inside and studied the room. There was a single bed covered with a navy comforter with baseballs on it, a dinosaur-shaped lamp and a collection of Hot Wheels cars that filled a shelf next to the bed.

He glanced at a desk and saw a stack of year-books and realized Barry collected them, even though he'd never graduated himself.

In the desk drawer, he found childlike drawings of a house with the sun shining above it, and stick figures portraying a family. Was Barry dreaming of finding a girl and marriage?

Chaz studied the photographs on the wall. He'd added a plastic rose above the girls' team from the crash, a tribute to the lost lives.

Frowning, Chaz dropped to his knees, checked under the bed and found the stash of girly maga-zines Mrs. Dothan had mentioned. He also dis-covered another box and pulled it out, then lifted the lid.

His gut clenched at what he found inside. Pic-tures of teenage girls outside the school. A pho-tograph of Ruth and Peyton from years ago when they'd worn harem costumes for a halftime show. Pictures of them dunking water over each other after a softball win.

A picture of the two of them at the swimming hole in their bikinis.

Then one of Tawny-Lynn in her bathing suit standing by the dock ready to dive into the lake.

Barry might not be dangerous, but the pictures were disturbing, and this spying had to stop.

He carried the pictures out to show Mrs. Dothan. She barely reacted when he laid them on the table. She simply lit another cigarette.

"Boys will be boys."

He opened his mouth to make a point, but the door bust open and Barry stumbled in.

Chaz frowned at the blood on Barry's shirt and hands.

Chapter Ten

When Barry saw Chaz, he turned and bolted. Chaz jumped up and caught him by the arm of his denim jacket. "Wait a minute, Barry."

"I didn't do anything wrong!" Barry shouted. "I didn't."

He gripped Barry by the arms. "How did you get that blood on your shirt and hands?"

"My nose. I crashed my bike into a tree."

"So it's your blood?"

Barry nodded but he was shaking, his eyes darting around for an escape. "Yeah, I didn't hurt nobody."

Mrs. Dothan stumbled over from her chair. "Barry, don't say anything."

Chaz reached for the strap of the camera slung over Barry's shoulder. "What were you doing in the woods? Were you taking pictures?"

"There's nothing wrong in taking pictures," Mrs. Dothan cut in.

Chaz flipped the camera over and hit the replay

button to view the pictures Barry had shot. An uneasy feeling traveled up his spine.

Various shots of Tawny-Lynn at the crash site. She looked so sad, so vulnerable, so tormented that his heart gave a painful tug.

"You took pictures of Tawny-Lynn this afternoon," he said. "I know how you obsess over girls," Chaz said. "Did you get mad when she told you to leave her alone?"

Barry started babbling about how he hit his nose on the tree again. "Didn't do anything wrong. Tawny-Lynn...wouldn't hurt her."

"You took pictures of my sister and Peyton Boulder years ago, Barry. I found them in your secret box."

"Pretty girls," Barry said. "I just like pretty girls."

"What do you like to do with them?" Chaz asked through gritted teeth.

"My boy doesn't do anything to the girls." Mrs. Dothan pulled Barry toward her. "He just likes to look."

Chaz reminded himself to be calm. He had no evidence that Barry had committed a crime. He removed his phone from his belt and retrieved the photos from Tawny-Lynn's porch. "See that threatening message, Barry. Are you sure you didn't get blood on you from the deer when you killed it and wrote on Tawny-Lynn's porch."

Barry's eyes widened in panic and a second later, he crumbled to the floor, wrapped his hands over his head and broke into incoherent sobs. "Don't kill deer, don't like blood. Stop it, stop it…."

"Sheriff, you need to leave," Mrs. Dothan said.

Chaz glared at Barry's mother. "If he hurt someone in the past, Mrs. Dothan, you're not helping him by protecting him."

"My son isn't dangerous," she cried as she stabbed her cigarette into the ashtray and knelt by her son. "Now get out!"

Chaz's heart hammered as Barry continued to wail. Was he innocent, or was he more dangerous than his mother and everyone thought?

Now that Tawny-Lynn was back and asking questions, she didn't want to stop. Seven years ago she'd been too traumatized and grief-stricken to think clearly. She barely remembered the sheriff talking to her or any of the leads he might have pursued in the investigation.

But she was sure someone—a male—had dragged her from the wreckage. Only no man had ever come forward to claim his hero status.

Which made everyone wonder if he had done something to Peyton and Ruth.

Seeing Cindy triggered memories of the other girls on the softball team. Not just the three who'd died, but the other players on the team who hadn't taken the bus that day. Two had been sick with a flu that had swept through the school, another girl had been out of town due to a death in the family, Judy

Samsung had been benched due to a broken arm and Rudy Henway and Paula Pennington had gone home with their parents because they'd planned to take the SATs the next morning.

Tawny-Lynn drove into town and stopped by the drugstore to pick up a refill of her migraine medication, then found a local phone book on the counter at the pharmacy. She grabbed it, slipped into a chair in the corner and thumbed through it, searching for each of the girls' names to see if any of them still lived in town.

Paula showed up under her maiden name, but not Rudy. But there was an ad for the Sports Barn, owned by Rudy Farnsworth. It had to be the same Rudy.

She punched Paula's number but the phone had been disconnected. She dialed the Sports Barn next and a woman answered.

"Hello, this is Rudy at the Sports Barn. What can I do for you?"

Tawny-Lynn panicked and hung up. She berated herself as she took a deep breath, then hurried out to the truck and drove to the shop on the edge of town. The ancient building had been renovated since she'd moved away, but as she entered, she realized the inside hadn't changed. Jerseys, shirts, trophies, bumper stickers and every other sports paraphernalia related to the local teams, both elementary, middle, high school and club teams were represented.

When she was small, she'd coveted the gleaming trophies in the glass cabinet.

"Be right with you." A young woman with striking red hair in a ponytail stood behind the counter writing up what she assumed was an order.

Tawny-Lynn remembered the tough-girl attitude Rudy had always emanated. She'd always wondered about the girl's home life.

A second later, the woman looked up, her amber eyes flashing with surprise. "Tawny-Lynn, you really are back?"

Tawny-Lynn shifted, her hands jittery although she didn't know why. "Not for long. Just to settle my daddy's ranch."

Rudy's expression softened. "Well, good luck with that."

"Thanks." Tawny-Lynn gestured at the jerseys and trophies. "So you own this place now?"

Rudy grinned. "Yes. I guess the tomboy in me never died." At the word *died,* she winced. "Sorry. I didn't mean it—"

"Don't apologize," Tawny-Lynn said. "I always loved this store. It's nice to know it's in the hands of someone else who appreciated it."

Rudy walked around the counter, and Tawny-Lynn noticed she was pregnant. "Oh, when's the baby due?"

"A couple of months," Rudy said. "I married a guy I met at A&M, Jo Farnsworth. He played football for the Aggies."

"Congratulations." A silence fell, and she fidgeted with one of the sweatbands on the shelf. At least Rudy had moved on and seemed happy.

Something she'd been unable to do. Even miles away in Austin, it was as if she were permanently stuck here in the past.

"I'm so sorry they never found Ruth or Peyton," Rudy finally said.

Tawny-Lynn gave a slight shrug. "I wish I could have helped more. Remembered..."

"It wasn't your fault," Rudy said. "Everyone was way too hard on you."

"Thanks." Unexpected tears burned Tawny-Lynn's eyes. "Can I ask you a question, Rudy?"

Rudy rubbed a hand over her belly, but a wary look pulled at her face. "What?"

"Did you ever hear my sister talking about a boyfriend after she broke up with J.J.?"

Rudy started refolding a stack of jerseys that were perfectly folded. "It was a long time ago, Tawny-Lynn, and you know Peyton and I weren't close friends. She was the pretty popular girl and I was...a dork."

Tawny-Lynn laughed for the first time in a long time as if she might have found a friend. "I always felt that way around her, too."

Rudy gave her a sympathetic look. "I always liked you. And I'll never forget that last game. You were awesome."

Tawny-Lynn blinked back more tears. For so

long, she'd associated everything about Camden Crossing with that horrible day. But there had been some good memories and people here.

"Thanks, I thought you were cool, too."

They both laughed.

"Good luck with the baby." A seed of envy sprouted inside Tawny-Lynn. She'd closed herself off from relationships for so long that she hadn't bothered to fantasize about marriage and a family of her own. She'd been too busy grieving the one she'd lost.

She turned to go, but Rudy rushed up behind her. "Tawny-Lynn, I…didn't want to say anything because…I don't want to speak bad about Peyton, but…"

"But what?" Tawny-Lynn clenched Rudy's hand. "Tell me. J.J. said he thought Peyton might have been involved with a married man."

Rudy's eyes flickered with regret. "I think she was, too."

"What makes you say that?"

"A couple of days before the accident, I left my bag in the locker room and went back to get it. I heard Peyton and Ruth talking."

"What were they saying?"

Rudy rubbed her swollen belly again. "Peyton was crying and said that she thought he'd leave his wife for her, but he wasn't going to. She sounded really upset."

"Did she say who the man was?"

Rudy shook her head. "No. Apparently he told her she'd better not tell anyone about the two of them, that he'd ruin her life if she did."

Tawny-Lynn's heart hammered. She had to find out who Peyton had been sleeping with. The man who'd made that threat could have killed her.

And if Ruth had known about him, he might have killed her to keep her quiet.

"MRS. DOTHAN," CHAZ said as he paused at the doorway. "If I find out you're lying to protect Barry, I'll come back and arrest you."

"I said get out!" Mrs. Dothan shouted over Barry's wails.

"I'm leaving, but watch your son. Taking pictures may seem innocent to you, but it also can be construed as stalking." He hesitated. "And, Barry, stay away from Tawny-Lynn Boulder."

He closed the door behind him, hoping they would heed his warning.

Tawny-Lynn's face flashed in his mind, and he itched to go see her. An itch he knew he should avoid scratching.

Because holding her felt too damn good. So good he wanted to hold her again.

Not going to happen.

His phone buzzed as he climbed into his car and drove back toward town. "Sheriff Camden."

"Sheriff, this is Sergeant Justin Thorpe with the Texas Rangers."

"What can I do for you, Sergeant Thorpe?"

"In the past month, two young women have gone missing in the counties next to Camden Crossing. Due to the cold cases in your town and Sunset Mesa, a special task force has been created to investigate the connection, if there is one."

"Tell me about the disappearances," Chaz said.

"A month ago, Carly Edgewater disappeared from a pep rally at the school where she teaches. So far, no one saw or heard anything."

"How about her family?"

"Prominent parents. They were at a charity fundraiser the night she went missing, so we've cleared them."

"Boyfriend or girlfriend trouble?"

"Not that we've uncovered, but I'm just starting the investigation."

"What about the second woman?"

"Name's Tina Grimes. Disappeared last week. Supposedly had a dentist appointment one morning, but never made it. When we checked, there was never a dentist appointment."

"So she lied? Why?"

"We don't know that yet. She supposedly had a boyfriend, but they broke up six months ago. Mom died last year of cancer, single father adores his daughter. He appears to be pretty distraught. Said the last few months had been difficult with his daughter. She was moody and depressed but refused therapy."

"So it's possible she ran off or hurt herself?"

"It's possible. But the sheriff never found a body and there was no suicide note."

Chaz pulled up to his office, parked and strode inside. "You've spoken with Sheriff Blair over in Sunset Mesa?"

"She's next on my list."

"So you think we're talking about one kidnapper?"

"Maybe. That's the reason for the task force, to coordinate efforts and see if we find a connection."

"If this perpetrator has been doing this for years and gotten away with it, he has to be pretty damn smart." Which would rule out Barry.

"He definitely knows how to stay under the radar."

His deputy must be making rounds as the office was empty. Chaz claimed his desk chair and turned to the computer. "Send me all the info you have on the cases. I'll compare it to our cold case: How old are these women?"

"Mid-twenties."

Hmm, maybe the cases weren't related. The first two victims had disappeared from Sunset Mesa when they were in their teens. These young women were in their twenties.

"Thanks. The more eyes we have on this, the better."

Chaz hung up and made himself some coffee while he waited on the information. When it came

in, he printed out copies of the files to take home
to study.

He jotted down some quick notes on the dates
of the disappearances, and frowned. Just as Sheriff
Blair mentioned, all the girls and these two women
had gone missing in the spring.

Was the time of year significant for a reason?
And if so, what the hell did it mean?

TAWNY-LYNN TACKLED her father's room when she
got home, but as she dumped liquor bottles and beer
cans into the trash, her conversations with Cindy
and Rudy replayed through her head.

Who was the older man Peyton had been in love
with?

Cigarette smoke permeated the air, so she gathered the bedding and towels in the bathroom and
piled them in the trash. She tackled her father's
closet next, a well of emotion bubbling inside her
as she folded his pants and shirts to donate to the
church. Some were too stained, tattered and smoke-
riddled to save, but she found two hats he'd bought
but never worn and Sunday ties that hadn't been
seen in a decade and added them to the church bag.

She flipped on the radio while she sorted and
cleaned, tuning in as the weatherman forecasted
rain by the weekend. Tomorrow she'd tackle the
outside of the ranch. She could finish cleaning and
do minor repairs on the rainy days.

Her shoulders ached with fatigue as she hauled

the bags out to the truck, then she scrubbed the walls and bathroom, determined to cleanse the smoky scent. But two hours later when her hands were practically raw, the scent still lingered.

Deciding she needed to clear the braided rug out, she rolled it up, dragged it outside and tossed it into the back of the truck to dispose of.

A noise sounded from the corner of the house, and her breath caught. Slowly she inched around the side to see what it was, and found a stray cat pawing at the ground by the old flowerbeds.

Relieved, she hurried back inside and locked the door. She finished in her father's room by taking down the ancient curtains that had turned from white to a yellowed brown, then tossed them into a trash bag.

She found another stack of mail on the desk and sorted through it. A crinkled envelope caught her eye, and she opened it, surprised to find an offer to buy the ranch from Chaz's father. Her eyes widened at the amount he'd offered. The letterhead held the bank's logo, and had been dated three weeks before.

Why would Mr. Camden want to buy the ranch?

Because he owned almost everything else in town.

Maybe he'd tried to run her father off like he'd done her because he reminded him of Ruth.

Did Chaz know about the offer?

She carried the envelope to the kitchen and dropped it into the basket with the unpaid bills, then returned to finish the bedroom. She found a shoebox of photos and put them in the den to sort through later.

Next she attacked the fireplace. It was full of old ashes and soot, so she swept it out and cleaned the hearth, then wiped down the fireplace tools. Then she swept and mopped the wood floor in her father's room.

Muscles aching, she stood back and admired her work. The house was old, but cleaning it made a huge difference. Exhausted, she climbed the steps, showered, then collapsed into bed.

Her landscape work was physical, but this heavy lifting had strained muscles she didn't even know she had.

She closed her eyes, praying the nightmares would leave her alone, and fell into a deep sleep. But sometime later, a noise startled her awake.

Cool air floated around her, giving her a chill. The house was old and drafty, but she remembered leaving the windows open in her father's room to air out the smoke, so she grabbed her robe, tugged it on and tiptoed down the stairs. She reached for the light to flip it on, but suddenly someone grabbed her from behind.

Tawny-Lynn screamed and threw her elbow back in defense, but her attacker threw her facedown and straddled her. She kicked and bucked, but he was heavier than her, and he pinned her to the floor.

Then he wrapped his hands around her throat, his fingers digging into her windpipe.

Chapter Eleven

Tawny-Lynn struggled to breathe, but her attacker tightened his grip and she gagged for air. Furious at herself for leaving the window open, she channeled that anger into adrenaline, shoved her hands beneath her chest and pushed herself up, bucking to throw her attacker off her.

The tactic worked, and he loosened his hold for a brief second, just long enough for her to crawl toward the fireplace. The poker was only inches away. If she could just reach it…

But he was fast. He gripped her ankle and tried to drag her away from it. She used her other foot to kick at him, then clawed her way toward the fire poker. A blow to her back made her cry out in pain, and tears burned her eyes.

But she blinked them back. She didn't intend to let this creep kill her.

She kicked backward again and heard his grunt as she connected with his nose. Panting for air, she scrambled to her knees and grabbed the poker.

Then she flipped around just as he charged

toward her. It was dark, but she squinted to see his face.

Impossible. He was wearing a ski mask, two dark eyes glaring at her as he heaved for a breath.

She clenched the fire poker in a white-knuckled grip and swung it just as she used to do the bat. He ducked to the side and she missed his head by a fraction of an inch. But the poker connected with his shoulder. He roared in anger and lunged to wrestle it from her, but she swung it toward his knees. She hit one and he crumpled with a curse.

Taking the fire poker with her, Tawny-Lynn jumped up and ran past him, stomach churning as she raced upstairs to get her phone. She stumbled once, but caught herself, then raced into her bedroom, grabbed her phone and locked herself in the bathroom.

Her hands trembled as she punched Chaz's number. God help her, she wished she'd grabbed her father's rifle from the closet. From now on, she'd sleep with it by the bed.

Downstairs, footsteps pounded, and she prayed he wasn't coming up the steps for her. The phone rang twice, then Chaz finally answered.

"Chaz, it's Tawny-Lynn. Someone's in the house. He tried to choke me."

"I'm on my way. Where are you?"

"Locked in my bathroom. Hurry..." She pressed her ear to the door to listen. "Oh, God, he's coming up the steps."

CHAZ GRABBED HIS GUN and raced to his car, fear for Tawny-Lynn spiking his adrenaline. He pressed the accelerator to the floor, tires squealing as he sped down the road toward White Forks.

Night cast shadows across the road, and he watched for cars in case Tawny-Lynn's intruder was escaping.

He hoped to hell the bastard had run and that Tawny-Lynn was safe.

He rounded the curve on two wheels, grateful he lived so close to the ranch and that hardly anyone was out on the road this late at night. His father had had a saying, that nothing good happened after midnight. One sentiment they agreed on.

A dark SUV flew past him, and he glanced back, wondering if it might be the intruder, but it had a Montana tag. Probably a tourist traveling through.

He swung the squad car down the drive to White Forks, then cut the siren, his headlights paving a path on the dark dirt drive. It was a moonless night, the stars hidden behind the ominous clouds that so far had held back their wrath.

He bounced over the ruts, his heart racing as he scanned the property. Except for Boulder's old pickup, there were no vehicles in sight.

Had the intruder parked down the road and hiked in through the woods?

He slammed his car to a stop, flipped off his lights and climbed out, easing his car door shut. He held his gun at the ready as he approached, checking in all directions for an ambush.

The sound of an animal scrounging through the woods echoed in the distance—or maybe it was Tawny-Lynn's attacker escaping.

He had to check the house first. Instincts on alert, he eased his way up the porch steps, mentally seeing that damned bloody deer carcass.

Apparently the threats had been real.

The front door was locked, so he jiggled it but the new dead bolt was in place. Damn. How had the intruder gotten in?

He rushed down the steps and walked around the side of the house until he found an open window in old man Boulder's room. Cursing beneath his breath, he climbed through the window, then tiptoed across the room, bracing his gun.

The room was clear. *Clean* and clear, he thought, shocked at how much work Tawny-Lynn had done in such a short time.

Holding his breath, he inched into the hall to the living room and kitchen and scanned the rooms. Though it was dark as hell, he didn't see or hear anything.

Tawny-Lynn said she was locked in her bathroom. He checked the laundry room off the kitchen and the back door. Still locked. The intruder had to have either left through the window or he was still upstairs.

Silence fell around him, tense and almost debilitating it was so thick with his own fear. He imagined finding Tawny-Lynn dead and his knees nearly caved beneath him.

He gripped the stair rail as he climbed the steps, then glanced in Peyton's room. Tawny-Lynn had obviously cleaned out the room, as well. The old posters, bedding and memorabilia had been packed up, the shelves empty. The room even smelled of Pine-Sol and furniture polish.

But no one was inside.

He inched toward Tawny-Lynn's room next, pausing to listen at the door. His mind traveled down a dangerous road, envisioning Tawny-Lynn's brutalized body, but he blinked to purge the disturbing images and turned the doorknob.

The door squeaked open, and he cut his eyes across the room. More shadows and darkness. He crept through the door, then checked the closet, relieved when no one jumped him, then rapped on the bathroom door.

"Tawny-Lynn, it's me, Chaz."

He waited a second, his breath tight, then rapped again. "Tawny-Lynn, it's me. The house is clear."

Suddenly the door swung open and Tawny-Lynn stood in front of him, a fire poker clenched in her hands, her face stark-white with fear.

TAWNY-LYNN WAS shaking so hard she could barely stand. She'd imagined her attacker breaking into the bathroom and finishing her off.

Then she'd never see Chaz again. Or find out what happened to her sister.

"He's gone. Are you all right?" Chaz asked in a gruff voice.

She nodded, but her throat was too thick to speak.

Then she didn't have to talk because Chaz stowed his gun in his holster, pulled her up against him and wrapped his arms around her. "Shh, it's okay now," he murmured against her hair.

"He tried to choke me," Tawny-Lynn whispered.

Chaz's breath brushed her cheek as he lifted her chin. "Did you see who it was?"

She shook her head, shivering as she remembered the man's hands gripping her throat. And his face…it was as blank as the man who'd dragged her from the fire.

Was it the same person?

"It was dark, and he wore a ski mask," she said. "All I saw were his eyes. I think they were brown."

Chaz examined her neck, his jaw tensing. "Did he say anything?"

"No…he just jumped me and threw me down."

He touched the handle of the fire poker. "You used this on him?"

She nodded, and he took it and dropped it to the floor. Then a slow smile spread across his face. "Good for you."

In spite of the tears pressing at the back of her

eyelids, she smiled. "I hit him in the shoulder and his knee."

"Then I'll look around in town for someone hobbling."

Tawny-Lynn laughed softly, and Chaz stroked her back with slow circles. "I'm sorry this happened, Tawny-Lynn." He pushed a strand of hair away from her cheek. "Sorry I wasn't here to protect you."

Tawny-Lynn laid her hand on his chest. His heart was racing, but he felt so strong beneath her that she felt his warmth seep into her, comforting.

"Thanks for coming."

Chaz squared his shoulders. "It's my job to protect the town."

So she was just a job to him? A way to find out what happened to Ruth...

She had to remember that.

She started to pull away, but he held her tight. "Wait, Tawny-Lynn, I didn't mean it like that."

Her gaze met his, tension rippling between them. "I understand, Chaz. I know I let everyone down."

"No, your father and everyone in the town let *you* down." He traced a finger along her jaw. "I let you down back then."

Tawny-Lynn's chest squeezed. "Chaz..."

"I promise I won't let you down now, though."

Tawny-Lynn couldn't remember when she'd had anyone to lean on. Anyone who cared about her.

But she couldn't lean on him. Could she?

Then he cupped her face between his hands, lowered his head and closed his mouth over hers. And she forgot about reservations and gave in to the moment.

CHAZ PRESSED HIS lips to Tawny-Lynn's mouth, his body hardening with arousal as she clung to him. He hadn't realized how much he wanted to protect her until he'd heard her terrified voice on the phone.

Or how much he wanted to be with her until he'd looked into those sea-green eyes.

Her soft whispered sigh urged him to deepen the kiss, and he flicked his tongue against her lips, coaxing them to open. He drove his tongue inside, tasting her, teasing her, aching for more.

He pulled her tighter against him, one hand going to her back to massage the tension from her shoulders. She raked a hand across his chest, sending fiery sensations through him that intensified his need.

Hunger and desire heated his blood, and he eased her back into the bedroom. But they nearly stumbled over the fire poker, reminding him of the reason he'd raced to her house like a madman.

Silently chiding himself, he looped his arms around her waist and ended the kiss. But he missed her already as she pulled back and looked up at him.

"Chaz?"

"I'm sorry, I shouldn't have done that."

"Why not?" Tawny-Lynn whispered. "Because of who I am?"

He shook his head. "No, because of who *I* am." Self-disgust underscored his tone. "I'm supposed to protect you, not take advantage of you."

"You didn't take advantage of me," she said softly.

He fisted his hands by his sides, desperately wanting to draw her back into his embrace. To kiss her and give her pleasure and alleviate the tormented look in her eyes,

But the only way to do the latter was to find out who'd tried to kill her.

And getting to the bottom of the cold case that had haunted Camden Crossing for seven years was the key to it.

"I should look for forensic evidence," he said. "Fingerprints."

"He wore gloves," she said, her finger automatically rubbing the bruise forming on her slender throat.

"Okay, but maybe he left fibers from his clothing, a hair, something that will help nail him when we catch him." He gestured around the room. "Was he in here?"

"No, he attacked me downstairs."

"He climbed in through a window in your father's room?"

She released a weary sigh. "I opened it earlier

to air out the room when I was cleaning. I was so exhausted I forgot to close it when I went to bed."

"Don't beat yourself up over it," Chaz said. "If he wanted to get in, he would have found another way."

She nodded in acceptance, then tightened the belt around her robe.

"Let me get my kit and camera. I want to take pictures of your neck and the crime scene, then I'll do a search."

"I'll meet you downstairs."

He hated to leave her for a second but duty called. So he jogged down the steps and retrieved his crime kit and camera.

Anger mounted as he tilted Tawny-Lynn's head backward and photographed the bruises on her neck. The imprint of a man's fingerprints discolored her skin. Only Tawny-Lynn said he'd worn gloves.

Still, they might be able to compare the sizes of the prints, so he took some close-up shots. Tawny-Lynn watched silently as he searched the room for forensics.

"You cleaned earlier?" Chaz asked.

She nodded.

He plucked a tiny black thread off the floor. "Then this must be from the intruder. I'll have the lab analyze it."

"It probably came off his ski cap."

"Maybe we can trace what kind of cap it is, where he bought it." It was a long shot, but he had to try it.

"I paid Barry Dothan a visit this afternoon," Chaz said.

Tawny-Lynn narrowed her eyes. "And?"

"He admitted to taking pictures of you and the other girls at school. But his mother claims he's innocent. She alibied him years ago."

"The sheriff really thought he could have hurt Ruth and Peyton?"

"He was a person of interest. But he became really upset when I accused him of stalking you. I don't know if he's dangerous, but I warned him to stay away from you."

"Thanks."

A frown puckered between his eyebrows. "Honestly though, judging from what I saw, I don't think he kidnapped our sisters. Over the years, he would probably have broken down and told someone."

"That's probably true," she said.

He shone a flashlight along the floor, looking for blood, an eyelash, anything that might help. "A Texas Ranger named Justin Thorpe called this afternoon. Two young women went missing from neighboring counties in the last two months. If the cases are connected, Dothan can't have done it. He only travels by bike."

"So he couldn't have gotten rid of Ruth's and Peyton's bodies if he'd killed them," Tawny-Lynn said.

"Right."

A heartbeat passed. "Chaz, this afternoon I talked to J.J. McMullen, Peyton's old boyfriend."

Chaz glanced up at her. "What did he have to say?"

"That Peyton dropped him for an older man. He thought the guy might have been married."

That was news to him. "Did he give you a name?"

She fidgeted with the belt of her robe. "No, he said he didn't know who it was. But it started me thinking about Peyton's other friends and that they might have known something about who she was seeing, so I went and talked to Cindy Miller, I mean Cindy Parker, and Rudy Farnsworth at the Sports Barn."

"Did they know who Peyton was seeing?"

"Not exactly. But Cindy got really nervous when I asked her. And Rudy said she'd heard Peyton crying, and telling Ruth that she thought her lover was going to leave his wife for her. But when Peyton pressed him, he threatened to ruin her life if she told anyone about them."

Chaz ran a hand through his hair. "There wasn't anything in the sheriff's report about a married lover."

"She obviously was with someone because I found condoms in her nightstand." Tawny-Lynn paused. "And if what Rudy said was true, this man might have panicked at the idea of Peyton exposing their affair."

"So he killed her to keep her quiet?"

"It's possible."

Chaz grimaced. Her theory made more sense than anything they'd considered so far. "Yeah, and if Ruth knew who he was, then that would have given him motive to kill her, too."

DAMN TAWNY-LYNN. She'd nearly broken his knee with that fire poker. She was tough—a fighter—that was for sure.

Just like she'd been on the softball field.

Not as soft and sweet as her sister. Or Ruth.

Ruth… Oh, beautiful Ruth.

He'd hated losing her. Had never meant for things to turn out the way they had…

The wind stirred the trees below, and now the curtains had been stripped in the old man's room, he could see every move the sheriff and Tawny-Lynn made.

Dammit. Camden was getting way too chummy with her. Didn't he have any allegiance to the town?

He'd watched the sheriff through his binoculars from his perch at the top of the hill and seen him making out with her.

That would be a complication. If the two of them got too close, he'd have to do something fast.

Killing Tawny-Lynn would be easy.

But killing the sheriff would be risky.

Still he'd do whatever he had to in order to protect his secret.

Chapter Twelve

Tawny-Lynn rubbed her aching back as she saw the wheels turning in Chaz's head. For the first time in years, she sensed he wasn't sure he wanted the answers.

Because they might find that Ruth and Peyton were both dead.

She'd long ago accepted that possibility. After all, if they had survived, why wouldn't one of them have contacted their families?

"I'm finished here if you want to go back to bed," Chaz said.

Tawny-Lynn shrugged. "I don't think I can sleep."

He gently touched her arm. "I'll stay downstairs and keep watch. Go get some rest."

"You don't have to stay, Chaz."

Worry knitted his brow. "Yes, I do, I'm the sheriff."

That's right. He was just doing his job. Maybe she had totally misread that kiss. But she could have sworn she'd felt his passion.

"I can't send this stuff to the lab until morning," he said. "Then I'm going to talk to Sheriff Simmons and see if he remembers any rumors about Peyton having an affair with a married man."

Good heavens. She'd known her sister was boy crazy and out of control those last few months, but how could she have slept with a man who already had a wife? Did he have children, too?

Did he still live in Camden Crossing?

If so, maybe he was worried that Tawny-Lynn knew his identity. Or that she'd find something in the house that would trigger her memory.

"Was there anything left from the fire?" she asked.

Chaz narrowed his eyes. "What do you mean?"

"Like Peyton's backpack. She liked to scribble J.J.'s name in her notebook. Maybe she scribbled this man's name in it, and the notebook was in her bag."

"I'll ask the sheriff," Chaz said. "You didn't find anything in her room?"

She hadn't searched every notebook. "Just the condoms. But I'll keep looking."

Chaz rubbed a hand down her arm. "This has been a helluva night for you. Go back to bed, Tawny-Lynn."

She was exhausted. But the thought of the nightmares returning—and a new one with the strangler in it—made her breath hitch.

She wanted to ask Chaz to go with her to bed. To hold her and comfort her through the night.

His gaze locked with hers for a moment, heat sizzling between them along with unanswered questions...and desire.

Desire was dangerous, though. It led to emotional entanglements like love, and she wasn't ready for that in her life.

Working with Chaz to find answers would have to be enough.

So she climbed the steps to her room and crawled into bed alone.

But she tossed and turned and sleep eluded her. Every time she closed her eyes she saw that masked man diving toward her. Felt his hands twisting her neck and squeezing the life out of her.

He hadn't succeeded tonight.

Which meant he would be back.

Would he kill her next time?

WATCHING TAWNY-LYNN retreat to her bedroom alone was one of the hardest things Chaz had done in a long time.

Ever since the day Ruth went missing, he'd blamed himself and turned his focus on finding out what happened to her. That was all tied to Tawny-Lynn, and her reappearance in Camden Crossing had given him hope.

But, hell. He was lying to himself if he didn't

admit that there was more. He was attracted to her. That kiss had only whetted his appetite for more.

Even worse, he liked her.

She was strong and gutsy, a fighter, a survivor in spite of all she'd endured. She didn't even seem to hate his family or the town, which she had every right to do.

And she wanted the truth as much as he did.

Only being this close to her, touching her, holding her, made him want something else just as much.

He wanted to keep her safe. Wanted to kiss her again and make love to her and...

He couldn't go there.

Instead, as he stood watch over Tawny-Lynn's house, he stewed over the information Tawny-Lynn had shared, mentally tossing around names of men in town who might have had an affair with Peyton.

He immediately dismissed the old-timers who hung out in front of the general store to play checkers. There were friends of his father's, but they were so much older he couldn't imagine Peyton being attracted to any of them.

Thanks to the new development on the lake and the mayor who'd spearheaded the project to renovate the exterior storefronts to give the town a cohesive Western look, the town had doubled in population in the last seven years.

New families and businesses meant progress for the town.

But whoever had taken Peyton and Ruth had lived in or near Camden Crossing seven years ago.

Keith Plumbing had been a suspect because he'd done odd jobs in Camden Crossing and Sunset Mesa, but he'd gone to Austin for a job that day. Only the job fell through. Plumbing claimed he was upset, bought a bottle of bourbon and spent the night in his truck.

But he had no one to corroborate his story. Still they'd had no evidence against him.

He tried to remember Plumbing's age and guessed he was early thirties now so he would have been young enough to attract a teen, yet old enough to be considered an older man by Peyton or Ruth.

Wind rattled the windowpanes in the house, and he combed through the downstairs rooms, making sure the locks were secure. His eyelids felt heavy so he brewed a pot of coffee and wandered outside to sit on the front porch.

Boulder had let the ranch go downhill. Not that it was a big working spread, but the place had potential. Two barns, a stable and riding pen. And enough pasture for a small herd of cattle.

An investor would probably sweep up the place, then Tawny-Lynn would be gone from his life forever.

An odd feeling pinched his gut at the thought.

She could have died earlier.

Hell. Someone still wanted her dead.

He sipped his coffee and watched as dawn

streaked the sky. Pinks and reds and oranges smothered the gray clouds from the night before, making the ranch look peaceful. Yet an eerie feeling washed over him, as if death had already taken hold of this land.

But he wouldn't let it claim Tawny-Lynn. She'd suffered enough. He'd protect her with his life.

TAWNY-LYNN WAITED until the sun had lifted into the sky, then finally slipped from bed. She was exhausted from staring at the ceiling and thinking about her attacker.

And the kiss she'd shared with Chaz.

She wanted to kiss him again.

But that would be risky to her heart. As soon as the ranch was ready to be put on the market, she'd return to her life. A life that didn't include Chaz.

Only could she leave with unanswered questions? And what if the man who'd attacked her last night had followed her?

She washed her face, brushed through her tangled hair and secured it into a ponytail. With rain on the horizon tomorrow, she dressed for yard work today.

The scent of coffee wafted up the stairs as she descended, and morning light washed over the den and kitchen. The place looked different now without the clutter and dust. Almost…homey.

With a little paint and some new furniture, someone *would* make it a home again. She could almost see a baby in a bassinet in the corner, a little boy with dark hair, running across the room with a football in his hand, a dog curled on a braided rug in front of the fireplace.

Good grief. The little boy she'd pictured had looked just like Chaz.

You are crazy, Tawny-Lynn. Crazy. Even if you and Chaz ever got romantic, his parents would never accept you.

She filled herself a coffee mug, then retrieved her father's rifle from the gun cabinet and set it by the stairs.

Then she found Chaz on the front porch in the swing with his own mug. Sunlight streaked his chiseled face, adding to his masculinity.

But when he glanced at her, shadows darkened his eyes.

"Did you sleep at all?" she asked.

The swing creaked as he pushed it back and forth with his feet. "No. Did you?"

"Not really." She sank into the swing beside him.

For a long moment, they sat in silence, just sipping their coffee and looking out over the ranch. The grass was dry, weeds choked the flowerbeds, and the barn and stables needed repairs.

So much to do.

Yet in the quiet of the morning, there was also something almost peaceful about the scenery. And something intimate about sharing it with Chaz.

Chaz slid his hand over hers, and Tawny-Lynn's

breath caught. Unable to help herself she curled her fingers into his. His touch felt warm, sensual, titillating.

"I'm headed out to see Sheriff Simmons today."

Anxiety wound Tawny-Lynn's stomach into a knot, any sense of peace evaporating.

"After what happened last night, I don't want to leave you alone, though. You can come with me."

Tawny-Lynn considered his suggestion, but being with him was playing havoc on her senses. "No, go ahead. I need to stay here and work outside today."

The sooner she fixed up the place, the sooner she could leave.

He slanted her a worried look. "It's not safe for you to be alone."

"No one is going to attack me in broad daylight. Besides, I found Daddy's rifle. I'll keep it with me outside just in case."

He arched his brows. "You know how to shoot?"

She smiled, grief twisting her heart. "That's the one thing my father and I did together. He taught me. I used to clean off the cans he set on the fence in ten seconds flat."

"There's a helluva difference between shooting cans and shooting a person."

She squeezed Chaz's hand, her gaze glued to his mouth. Her body ached to be held, her lips yearned to touch his again. But the memory of that man's hands around her throat as he tried to strangle the life out of her, taunted her.

"I can do it if I have to."

He put his coffee mug on the porch floor, then took hers and did the same. Then he lifted a finger and traced it along her jaw. "You're strong, Tawny-Lynn. I admire that about you."

She shook her head. "I'm not strong, Chaz. If I was, I'd be able to remember, to see that man's face."

A silence fell between them, fraught with old pain and anguish.

Chaz leaned forward and kissed her again. This kiss was tender, sweet, full of passion and promise. Tawny-Lynn leaned into him, savoring his taste and wishing it could last forever.

He probed her lips apart with his tongue and deepened the kiss, their tongues dancing in tandem. Raw need flooded Tawny-Lynn.

She wanted more, to take him upstairs and get naked with him.

But he ended the kiss, then pulled away and stroked her cheek again. "Are you sure you can handle the rifle?"

She smiled. "I won the skeet shoot at the county fair when I was twelve."

"I wish I'd seen that."

Maybe if she stuck around she'd show him.

She froze. Where had that thought come from? She would never stay in Camden Crossing.

He squeezed her hand again then stood. "Call me if you need me. I'll check in after I talk to Simmons."

She lifted their joined hands, then kissed his palm. "Thanks for coming last night, Chaz. And for staying."

He paused, his eyes flickering with emotions she couldn't define. Worry? Hunger? Desire?

"I promise you I'll find the man who hurt you."

She licked her bottom lip, hating the reminder as he walked to his car. But for once in her life, she didn't feel alone. Chaz would keep his promise.

Still, she grabbed the rifle for protection as she headed outside to work in the yard.

As MUCH AS Chaz hated to leave Tawny-Lynn, he wanted to talk to Simmons and question Keith Plumbing, and thought it might be best if she wasn't with him for the latter in case Plumbing admitted to an affair and disparaged Peyton.

But tension coiled inside him. Although her attacker most likely wouldn't come back during the day, Chaz didn't like the fact that someone wanted to hurt her.

He drove home and showered, then went straight to Sheriff Simmons's place, a rustic log cabin he'd built for retirement on the creek. Gravel crunched beneath his boots as he made his way to the front door. The sound of water gurgling over rocks echoed from behind the cabin.

He knocked again but no one answered, so he walked to the side of the cabin and spotted Simmons sitting on a rock, holding a fishing pole.

Simmons glanced up at him, squinting at the bright morning sun.

"Hey," Chaz said. "Are they biting?"

Simmons chuckled. "No, but I'm not giving up."

Chaz gestured at the bait bucket on the ground. "Looks like you're enjoying retirement."

Simmons shrugged. "Gets lonely sometimes. This was mine and Dorothy's dream. Not so much fun alone."

A pang stabbed at Chaz's heart. Simmons and his wife had been married thirty years, but the very year Simmons retired, he lost his wife to cancer.

"But you didn't drive out here to listen to me complain," Simmons said. "What's up, Camden?"

Chaz explained about Tawny-Lynn being back in town and the trouble. "Someone attacked Tawny-Lynn last night."

Simmons whistled. "That poor girl. She's been through hell." He wiped his forehead with the back of his hand. "Her daddy treated her like Peyton's disappearance was her fault. I wasn't surprised when she didn't want a memorial service."

Sympathy for Tawny-Lynn swelled inside Chaz, mingling with his growing admiration for her.

Chaz sat down on another rock and watched the birds dipping toward the water.

Simmons pulled in his pole, checked the bait then cast it again. "So what can I do for you?"

"Tawny-Lynn talked to a couple of former classmates and thinks that Peyton might have been having an affair with a married man. Did anyone mention that when you investigated?"

Simmons scowled. "No. I talked to a few of the kids at the memorial services, but everyone said Peyton was dating J.J. McMullen. Your folks said Ruth wasn't involved with anyone."

Chaz picked up a rock and skipped it across the water. "What if J.J. was pissed off about the breakup? Maybe he followed the bus and ran it off the road, then abducted Peyton and Ruth?" After all, he'd been strong even at eighteen. He could have subdued the girls one at a time.

"That's possible, although I remember talking to J.J. and he was pretty broken up. He had an alibi, too. One of the cheerleaders said he was with her during the time of the crash."

"He could have convinced the girl to lie for him," Chaz suggested.

Simmons shrugged. "I suppose that's true."

"Did any of the teenagers mention that someone had a grudge against Peyton or Ruth?"

"Not that I recall. At the time, we assumed the case was connected to the missing girls from Sunset Mesa."

"We have to consider all the possibilities," Chaz said. "Did anyone go missing about that time? A man, I mean?"

"No. I checked in case one of the girls ran off with someone but no names came up."

He'd have a chat with J.J. McMullen. If he had

done something to the girls, maybe guilt had set in and he'd be ready to confess.

If not, he'd look at Plumbing again.

Hell. He understood the reason the case had gone cold. One question only led to another, and different theories where they'd chased lead after lead ended up yielding no results.

Tawny-Lynn seemed to be the only one who might have seen something.

But that secret was locked in her head.

The very reason someone wanted her dead.

TAWNY-LYNN STACKED the dishes in the dishwasher, retrieved the few gardening tools she could find in her father's shed, stuffed an old high-school ball cap on her head and walked outside. She surveyed the front property and realized the most she could do short-term was to clean out the weed-infested flowerbeds and plant some roses.

That would require a run to the lawn-and-garden supply store for compost and a good sprayer. But first she needed to weed the beds in front and the one on the side of the house.

She yanked on gardening gloves, knowing she had to take advantage of the early-morning temperatures before the hot Texas sun climbed the sky.

She yanked and pulled and tore the weeds from the two beds flanking the porch steps, then checked the pH level of the soil. Yes, it definitely needed the nutrients provided by bonemeal so she mentally added that to her list.

Perspiration beaded on her forehead, and she swiped at it with the back of her sleeve, dumped the weeds into the wheelbarrow, then hauled it around to the right side to work on the last flowerbed. She'd probably need a new trellis here and would put climbing roses, maybe a mixture of red, yellow and pink to add color against the faded white house.

The entire structure needed painting, but she didn't have the money for that. The new owners could fix it up the way they wanted.

A momentary pang of sadness assaulted her as she actually imagined the for-sale sign in the front yard.

Good grief. She couldn't get sentimental now. This place would be an albatross around her neck if she kept it.

And too much of a reminder of the family she'd lost.

Something sparkled in the sunlight and she squatted down and realized it was a bracelet nearly buried in the dirt.

With gloved hands, she brushed away dirt until the bracelet was uncovered fully, then picked it up. Her heart slammed against her rib cage as she turned it around and studied the charms.

Both Peyton and Ruth had worn charm bracelets. Her sister's favorite charm had been a heart she'd said her secret boyfriend had given her. At the time, she'd thought Peyton was joking about the boyfriend.

But this bracelet didn't have a heart charm. Instead, there was a tulip, a cougar for Camden Creek Cats, a telephone, pair of red high heels and a small key, which said Key to My Heart.

This bracelet had belonged to Ruth.

Her heart pounded. Why was it here in the old flowerbed? Had Ruth lost it one day when she was on the ranch?

Although Ruth and Peyton never worked in the garden. That had been her job.

Only, she'd lost interest for a while after the accident.

She held the bracelet up to the light, her eyes widening as she spotted a dark stain on the band of the bracelet. It looked like…blood.

Her imagination went wild. But reality interceded, and she realized Ruth could have lost it months before the accident. An animal or even the wind could have tossed it in the dirt. In fact, she'd seen the cat pawing in this flowerbed the night before.

She tucked it in her pocket. She'd save it and give it to Chaz. He'd probably want to keep it.

Curious still as to how it had come to be in the flowerbed, she raked her hand through the weeds.

The ground was uneven. Slightly curved at the top almost like a…grave.

Pulse clamoring, she grabbed the shovel and

began to dig. One shovel of dirt, another, a third…
and the shovel tip hit something.

She knelt to examine it and gasped.

Dear God, no…

The shovel had hit bone.

Chapter Thirteen

After leaving Simmons, Chaz stopped by the butcher shop. J.J. stood behind the counter, his apron bloody from cutting meat for the morning shopping crowd.

He'd always thought it odd that J.J., who'd been a popular football player, had come back to help run his father's store. He'd called his deputy on the way over and asked him to run a check on McMullen and had learned some interesting stuff.

The former football star had a record.

J.J. looked up at him, a wary look creasing his beefy face. He handed the woman her order, then she went to the register to pay J.J.'s father.

Chaz crossed his arms. "We need to talk."

J.J. shot his father a wary look, but his father motioned for him to take a break.

J.J. led him through the back work area, and Chaz grimaced at the bloody meat on the stainless-steel tables. The meat-cooling locker stood to the right.

A good place to hide a body.

"What do you want?" J.J. asked.

Chaz decided to use the direct approach. "Someone tried to kill Tawny-Lynn Boulder last night. Where were you?"

The man's mouth fell open, then he shut it, his eyes livid. "You think I tried to hurt her? Why the hell would I do that?"

"Just asking." Chaz lifted his brows, waiting.

J.J. ran a hand over his apron and heaved a breath. "Listen, it wasn't me."

"You know who it was then?"

"No. I just mean I wouldn't hurt Tawny-Lynn."

"You left college because you were arrested for assaulting a girl."

Shock streaked J.J.'s face. "That was bull. Someone at a party gave this girl some coke. She went crazy and accused me of coming on to her. But I never touched her."

"Then why did you leave school?"

"Because her father was rich and, at that point, I'd blown out my knee and couldn't play ball." He gestured at the butcher shop. "As you can see, my family doesn't have money like yours. I couldn't afford a fancy lawyer, so the court-appointed attorney, some kid barely out of diapers, talked me into a plea."

Chaz gritted his teeth. "What about Peyton Boulder? She left you for another guy, an older man. That make you mad?"

J.J. glared at him. "Yeah, it made me mad. But not enough to kill her. For God's sake, I loved her."

"All the more reason for you to try to win her back. Maybe you chased down the bus, accidentally hit them, then pulled her out. When she wouldn't go with you, you lost your temper."

"That's not true. I wasn't even in Camden Crossing that day," J.J. growled. "I was…never mind."

"Where were you?" Chaz asked.

J.J. looked down at his apron, then his blood-stained hands. For God's sake, he could have cut the girls up to pieces and stored them in his father's meat locker until all the commotion died down.

"Where were you?"

"I don't have to tell you anything," J.J. said.

"Sheriff Simmons said one of the cheerleaders gave you an alibi. If I talk to her, is she going to change her story?"

A frisson of fear streaked J.J.'s face. "If you're going to arrest me, I want a lawyer."

A bold move since he'd just claimed that his first one had failed him.

Chaz jerked him by the collar. "If you're innocent and have nothing to hide, you'll tell me. Then I can eliminate you as a suspect."

J.J.'s nostrils flared. "Coach caught me smoking weed and threatened to cut me from the team unless I went for treatment. I was in a drug rehab class that day. *All* day."

That would be easy to check.

Chaz had one more question. "Did Peyton tell you the name of the man she was seeing?"

J.J. hissed between his teeth. "No. But she said she was going to marry him, and he'd give her everything she ever wanted. Things I couldn't."

J.J.'s angry gaze flattened, grief replacing the anger. "I didn't hurt Peyton," he said. "Besides, if I knew the jerk she was seeing, I would have gone after him, not her."

Chaz's phone buzzed, and he quickly checked the number. Tawny-Lynn.

"Don't leave town," he told J.J. as he walked away to answer the call.

"Chaz," Tawny-Lynn cried. "You have to come quick."

He jumped in his car and flipped the engine. "What's wrong? Did the guy come back?"

"No," Tawny-Lynn said, her voice cracking. "I found a body on the ranch."

Dread balled in his belly. If it was on White Forks, odds were that it was Peyton. And if Peyton was buried there, would Ruth be there, too?

Tawny-Lynn's hand trembled as she jammed her phone into her pocket. She couldn't take her eyes off the grave.

For a moment, she'd hoped, prayed, that the bones belonged to their old dog who'd died when she was a freshman in high school. But she'd raked enough dirt away to see one of the blankets they used to keep in the barn in the hole.

Someone had used the blanket to wrap the body in.

And judging from the length of the grave, a human body lay inside.

A noise from the woods startled her, and she grabbed the rifle and swung it toward the direction of the sound. Seconds later, a baby doe scampered away, and she blew out a breath of relief.

Damn. Her hands were shaking so badly that if that had been her attacker from the night before, she would have missed him by a mile. That is, if she managed to fire a shot before he jumped her.

Struggling to calm herself, she walked back to the porch and sat down on the steps. But she kept her eyes peeled for trouble, the rifle in her hands.

Her phone buzzed again, and she saw it was the auto-shop number, so she snapped it up with one hand.

"Tawny-Lynn, about your car…"

God, she'd forgotten to call him. "Yes?"

"I had to realign it and we pounded out the dent. I figure we'll check out the brakes while it's here. You can pick it up tomorrow."

"Okay, great. Thanks."

An engine roared down the driveway and she looked up, grateful to see Chaz zooming up to the house. He screeched to a stop, jumped out and ran toward her, then eased the rifle from her hands and laid it on the porch. He gripped her arms. "Where's the body?"

Tawny-Lynn swallowed hard and pointed toward the flowerbed. "I was digging up weeds to plant some roses when the shovel hit something."

Chaz squeezed her hands. "Stay here. I'll take a look."

"Chaz?"

"Yeah?"

"At first I thought it might be the dog we used to have, but…the body's wrapped in a blanket from the horse barn. And the grave…it's too big."

His eyes flickered with myriad emotions, then he walked around the side of the house. Tawny-Lynn dropped her head in her hands, her mind spinning.

Her father and sister had argued the night before Peyton went missing. But he hadn't hurt her….

She'd been in that bus accident. So how would Peyton's body have ended up here?

DREAD BALLOONED IN Chaz's chest as he rounded the house and stooped by the flowerbed. Tawny-Lynn was right.

The hole was a grave, although she'd barely uncovered enough for him to see the size. Odds were, though, that her sister was buried here and that a domestic dispute between father and daughter had occurred.

Hadn't Tawny-Lynn been through enough without finding Peyton's body on her homestead?

Still, the grave triggered more questions.

How had the body gotten here? He tried to piece together a possible scenario in his mind. Her father had discovered Peyton was having an affair with a married man, then found Peyton at the crash site and brought her to the ranch and...what? Killed her? That didn't make sense. Especially when police were crawling over the crash site and Tawny-Lynn had been injured.

He'd have to check and see what time Boulder had shown up at the hospital.

He phoned the crime team from the county, knowing he needed help. With a body this decomposed, they needed a forensic specialist and an M.E., all with skills he didn't possess.

While he waited on them to arrive, he strode to his car, retrieved his camera and snapped some pictures of the scene, capturing the grave, blanket and bone poking through the soil. When he finished, he found Tawny-Lynn still sitting on the steps, her forehead creased with anxiety.

"The M.E. and crime lab techs will be here soon. They'll transport the body to the morgue for an autopsy."

She nodded, but she looked numb. He took her hands in his and realized they were icy cold, so he rubbed them between his own to warm them.

"I'm so sorry, Tawny-Lynn."

"I'm going to make some coffee," she said as if rallying. "I have a feeling it's going to be a long afternoon."

He wished he could make this nightmare easier for her, but he couldn't. And if Peyton was in the ground, where was Ruth? They'd assumed all these years that the same man had abducted the two of them.

Now he didn't know what to think.

THE CRIME UNIT AND M.E. arrived, and Tawny-Lynn stepped back outside for introductions. "Lieutenant Levi Gibbons," a big, dark-haired man said. "I'm with the crime lab and M.E.'s office." He gestured toward two younger men, a blond with a buzz cut and a brown-haired guy with a goatee. "This is Seth Arnaught and Corey Benson."

Chaz introduced himself, and Tawny-Lynn shook their hands. "There's coffee and sandwiches inside whenever you want them."

The lieutenant removed his sunglasses and leveled Tawny-Lynn with a concerned look. "You found the body, ma'am?"

Tawny-Lynn nodded and lifted her chin. Some of the color had returned to her face, but her eyes still looked listless. In shock.

But she was trying her damnedest not to show any weakness.

"I came back to the ranch to fix it up to sell it.

I was digging through the flowerbeds when the shovel hit bone."

Another man, mid-fifties with silver hair, emerged with his own team. "I'm the chief medical examiner, Stony Sagebrush."

Another round of introductions were made, then Chaz asked, "Are you men familiar with the case of the two girls who disappeared from Camden Crossing seven years ago?"

They indicated that they were.

"You think this is one of the girls?" Lieutenant Gibbons asked.

Tawny-Lynn cleared her throat. "Yes. Maybe my sister, Peyton."

"What would make you say that?" Lieutenant Gibbons asked. "Didn't your father and sister get along?"

Tawny-Lynn gave Chaz a pleading look.

"Her father liked to drink," Chaz said. "But Peyton went missing from the bus accident, so there are a lot of missing pieces to the puzzle."

"All right, let's get to work," Gibbons said. "No use speculating until we verify whose body it is."

They all agreed, and Chaz led the crime team and M.E. around the side of the house to the grave. They snapped photographs of the house, surrounding property and gravesite before the team exhumed the body.

Tawny-Lynn remained on the porch with a cup of coffee, a faraway look in her eyes.

"You said there were two missing girls?" Lieutenant Gibbons glanced across the property. "Do you think the other girl is buried here somewhere?"

Chaz swallowed the lump in his throat. "I don't know. If Peyton's father took her from the accident and killed her, it was probably in a fit of rage. I still can't figure out how he'd have gotten her to leave the accident scene anyway. Tawny-Lynn was hurt and rushed to the hospital, and there were rescue workers and law enforcement officers everywhere."

"Maybe the two girls escaped but were disoriented and wandered away from the scene. Then Boulder showed up and found them?"

"I suppose it's possible, although there are still too many holes in the theory."

"If I were you, I'd organize a search party to comb this ranch just in case," Lieutenant Gibbons suggested.

Chaz considered the idea. "I'll get right on it."

He walked back to the porch to ask Tawny-Lynn's permission before he phoned his deputy to organize the search.

She wiped at a tear that had escaped as he climbed the steps. When he explained the lieutenant's suggestion, she readily agreed. "We said we wanted answers, didn't we?" She sipped her coffee, her eyes blank. "We may not like what we find, Chaz."

He couldn't argue with that. But still they had to follow through. So he went inside, poured himself a mug of coffee and phoned his deputy.

Within an hour, ten men showed up to ride the property. While they did, Chaz went to search the barn and stables.

If someone had been in a hurry to dispose of a body, that would have been a likely hiding spot.

TAWNY-LYNN REMEMBERED the bracelet she'd found and fingered it as Chaz headed out to the barn. The deputy and the search party rode out, half on horses they'd brought in trailers, the other half in Jeeps and SUVs.

She needed to give the bracelet to Chaz. But seeing it would upset him and raise questions as to how it had come to be in the flowerbed.

Because Ruth was buried in the ground there instead of Peyton?

That made absolutely no sense. Her father would never have hurt Ruth. And if Peyton had survived, she would have never left her best friend.

Besides, showing Chaz the bracelet now would only make him feel the unbearable sense of anguish and panic that had seized her chest at the thought of the body belonging to Peyton.

She cared too much about him to put him through that torture until they knew for sure.

She stuffed it back into her pocket. She would give it to him after they received the M.E.'s report.

Decision made, she went inside, grabbed more trash bags and retreated to her room. She'd cleaned out her father's and Peyton's rooms, now it was time to do the same to hers. The sooner she did, the sooner she could leave this godforsaken ranch and town.

She plowed through the closet, yanking out clothes she hadn't seen or worn in years. T-shirts, jeans, skirts, shoes…everything went into the bags. When the closet was empty, she attacked the desk in the corner, embarrassed when she found an old notebook where she'd scribbled Chaz's name a dozen times like a love-struck teenager.

He hadn't given her the time of day back then, but she thought he'd hung the moon.

She still did, dammit. He'd only grown more handsome and stronger in her eyes.

Suddenly a board squeaked and a man's voice boomed from the doorway. "What are you doing, Ms. Boulder?"

Tawny-Lynn swung her head toward the lieutenant. "Just cleaning out my old room."

"Stop." He strode forward and snatched the notebook from her, raising his eyebrows in question at her silly teenage scrawls. She didn't realize Chaz was with him until she heard his quick hiss of breath.

Embarrassment heated her cheeks. "That was a long time ago, in high school."

"This house, the property, it may have been the scene of a crime. Are you trying to get rid of evidence?"

Shock slammed into Tawny-Lynn. "No, of course not. I told you, I'm getting the property ready to sell."

"We'll need to search your room, your father's and sister's," the lieutenant said.

Tawny-Lynn froze. "I…already cleaned out their rooms."

"Really. First you throw things out, then you report a body." Lieutenant Gibbons's eyes flared with suspicion. "It sounds like you're trying to get rid of evidence."

Panic fluttered in her belly. "That's not true." She stood, bracing her hands on her hips. "I didn't know that body was out there, Lieutenant. I only came home because my father died and I wanted to sell this place."

The lieutenant indicated the notebook. "Were you jealous of your sister, Ms. Boulder? Did something happen between the two of you and things got out of hand?"

"That's enough," Chaz cut in. "My sister and hers were alive when they boarded the bus after the softball game that day. Tawny-Lynn was seriously injured and transported to the hospital from the scene. There's no way she could have—or would have—hurt either Peyton or Ruth."

Tawny-Lynn gave Chaz a grateful look, but she sensed the lieutenant wasn't satisfied. "Maybe not, but she could have covered for her father all these years."

Anger railed inside her. She'd heard those accusations before.

"I suggest you wait on the porch until my men search the house." He gave her a warning look. "And tell me where your father's and sister's things are. My men will need to search those, as well."

Tawny-Lynn glared at him. "I took the trash to the dump, the clothes to the church."

He spoke into the mike at his lapel and ordered one of his guys to go to the church.

"Come on, Tawny-Lynn." Chaz took her by the arm and escorted her down the steps and onto the front porch, while the men went to work in her house.

She fell into the porch swing and stared at the sky while the crime team searched her house and toolshed and went to confiscate the items at the church. The hours dragged by while the men from town combed her property.

Emotions pummeled Tawny-Lynn, and by the time the team had finished and left, dusk had long set and night had fallen. She felt defeated, numb, helpless.

And furious that once again her life was being turned upside down, her innocence questioned.

"It'll be morning before we receive the M.E.'s report, if then," Chaz said as the last of the search party left. Thankfully they hadn't found another grave or body.

He handed her a drink, a shot of scotch from the only bottle she'd saved because it hadn't been opened. She willingly took it and downed it, needing the warmth of the alcohol to stir her blood.

He brought her another and kept one for himself, then sank onto the porch swing beside her. The creak of the swing rocked the night as they finished their drinks in silence.

"I'm going to shower," she said, suddenly feeling dirty and as if a bath could wash away the shame of what had happened today.

He nodded. "I'll keep watch."

"You don't have to stay, Chaz."

"I'm not leaving you tonight," Chaz said gruffly.

She didn't have the energy to argue. Worse, she didn't want to be alone.

So she headed up the steps, dropped her clothes on the floor by the bed, then grabbed her robe. But as soon as she climbed into the shower, the floodgates unleashed. She cried for Peyton and her father and herself.

And for Chaz and what she wanted between them that could never be.

CHAZ HEARD TAWNY-LYNN crying after he'd locked up and walked upstairs. Finding the body had shaken them both up, but having Gibbons accuse her of protecting her father had obviously resurrected bad memories of the past and driven her over the edge.

He removed his holster and placed his weapon on the nightstand, the rational side of his brain ordering him to go back downstairs. Tawny-Lynn needed rest, sleep, to be alone.

But he needed to be with her. To hold her and assuage her pain.

The sound of the shower water faded, then seconds later, the door squeaked open. Steam oozed from inside, then Tawny-Lynn appeared in the doorway, her damp hair hanging in ringlets around her pale face, her eyes haunted.

She looked so beautiful, though, that his gut clenched.

She glanced at the bed, then into his eyes. "What are you doing?"

He stood and walked over to her. "I told you I wasn't leaving you tonight."

Her lower lip trembled, then hunger flared in her eyes. That moment of raw emotion was all he needed.

He pulled her into his arms and closed his mouth over hers. She clawed at his shirt, popping buttons in her haste, then raked her hands over his chest as he plunged his tongue into her mouth.

Chapter Fourteen

Chaz cradled Tawny-Lynn's face between his hands, deepening the kiss as he backed her toward the bed. Her damp hair brushed his cheek as he lowered his head to nibble at the sensitive shell of her ear, then he dipped lower, trailing kisses down her neck.

The bruising from her attacker angered him, and he traced a finger gently over the imprint of the man's fingers.

No one would ever hurt her again. Not as long as he was around.

She threaded her fingers into his hair, need igniting between them, and he raked a finger across her nipple through her robe. She whispered a pleasured sigh, then pushed his shirt to the floor.

Breathing in her feminine scent was intoxicating and stirred his hunger to a burning fever. He parted the top of her robe and kissed her delicate neckline, dipping lower to tug one bare nipple between his teeth.

She groaned and arched her back, then reached

for his belt. Her fingers made quick work of unfastening it, then she unsnapped his jeans. His length hardened, bulging against his fly.

He couldn't remember the last time he'd been with a woman. But even then, he hadn't wanted her the way he wanted Tawny-Lynn. He laved one breast, moving slowly to the next and suckling her nipple until she cried out and shoved his jeans down his hips.

He pulled away long enough to step out of them, one hand working the belt of her robe. He slipped the knot free, his breath catching as he stripped it and feasted on her naked body.

"You're lovely," he whispered.

Tawny-Lynn blushed. "Chaz—"

"Shh. I've been thinking about this for a long time."

"Me, too."

Her whispered confession sparked a fiery heat in his belly, and he eased her down on the bed and climbed on top of her. Her skin felt silky soft and tasted like berries as he kissed her again, tracing his tongue from her neck down her breasts to her center. She pulled at his arms, but he parted her legs and dove his tongue into her core.

Tawny-Lynn's fingers dug into his hair and she moaned, her body shuddering as she succumbed to the pleasure. Her sweet release dampened his tongue, making him even more desperate to be inside her.

She shivered, twisting at the sheets as he shed his boxers and grabbed a condom from his pocket. Desire flared in her eyes as she helped him roll it on, then she curled her fingers around his thick length and stroked him.

He grabbed her hand, determined to prolong their pleasure, then pushed her legs apart with his thigh and settled between her.

"Chaz," she murmured in a hoarse whisper.

"I want you, baby." His fingers toyed with her sensitive nub for a moment, then he deftly replaced his fingers with his sex and guided himself to her damp center. She arched her back, lifting her hips to accommodate him as he thrust inside her.

She was warm, soft, sensational.

Fire rose inside him, creating a burning ache that only she could quench, and he pulled out and thrust into her again, filling her over and over until she cried out his name again, and he lost himself inside her.

TAWNY-LYNN'S BODY quivered. She'd had sex a couple of times, both meaningless encounters, but none that had aroused her emotions and stirred her body to the heights Chaz had.

Because she was falling in love with him.

Panic tightened her chest. She couldn't be in love with Chaz. She had to leave Camden Crossing soon, and he…would stay here with his family.

But he rolled them to the side, wrapped his arms

around her and she nestled into him and closed her eyes.

Tomorrow she'd face reality. Tonight she wanted to lie in his arms, hold him and pretend that they had a future together.

But in the back of her mind, the truth gnawed at her. The M.E. would determine the identity of the body found on White Forks. They still had questions. Answers to find.

A killer to track down.

But Chaz kissed her again, and she forgot about the body and murder and all the reasons she and Chaz shouldn't be together. She wanted him tonight and he wanted her.

That was all that mattered.

So she gently stroked the side of his jaw and teased him with kisses along his neck and chest. Moments later, the passion ignited between them again, and they made love a second time—this time long and slow, exploring each other's bodies.

And when she finally fell asleep, she dreamed about a happy time, where she and Chaz were riding on horseback across the ranch with the wind blowing, flowers blooming and their future bright and happy—a future they would spend together.

THE SOUND OF his phone buzzing woke Chaz long before he wanted to get up or leave the bed. He reached across Tawny-Lynn and retrieved it from the nightstand, his stomach knotting at the sight of the M.E.'s number.

Dragging on his jeans, he walked to the window and looked out as the call connected. "Sheriff Camden speaking."

"This is Dr. Sagebrush. I have some news about the body."

Chaz glanced back at Tawny-Lynn and watched her roll over and stretch. Her long hair was splayed across the pillow, her beautiful breasts exposed as the sheet slipped down to reveal nipples, tight and begging for attention.

He wanted to hang up the damn phone and go back to bed with her. To make love and bury themselves in each other until they forgot about the past.

But he couldn't do that.

"Yeah?"

"Maybe we should meet, Sheriff. I hate to give bad news over the phone."

"Look, Tawny-Lynn and I have both been in the dark for years. Just tell me—did the body belong to her sister?"

Tawny-Lynn must have heard him because she sat up, rubbing her eyes with a frown.

"No, I checked dental records, Sheriff. The body is not Peyton Boulder." He paused and Chaz's heart hammered.

"Then who was it?"

"It was your sister, Sheriff."

The room seemed to spin out of control. Hot air swirled around Chaz, nearly suffocating him.

He blinked, swallowed hard, leaned his head against the windowpane. Outside the sun was shining, but he couldn't see anything but those bones.

Then his sister's face when she was ten and had bounced into the room to beg him to take her fishing. Pain, deep and raw, immobilized him as more images of Ruth flashed through his head.

Ruth at six with her gap-toothed smile, holding her doll and standing in front of the Christmas tree. Ruth at twelve when she'd taken up in-line skating and broken her arm. Ruth at her first school dance where he'd watched over her like a hawk to make sure the boy she was with didn't make a play to get her behind the bleachers.

All these years he'd hoped…what? That Ruth would be alive and living somewhere doing what? He'd known this was probably the outcome.

Except, why the hell had her body been found on White Forks?

"Sheriff?"

He scrubbed a hand down his chin, struggling for composure. "Yeah, I'm here. You're sure about this?"

"Yes. I have both dental and medical records. She had an old injury, a broken arm?"

"Yes."

"I'm sorry, Sheriff."

His detective skills finally breached through

his shock. "Do you know how long she's been buried there?"

"About seven years."

So she had never really escaped or left Camden Crossing. "What was the cause of death?"

"Judging from contusions on the skull, she died of a blow to the head. It looks like from a sharp object."

"A sharp object?"

"Yes, but I can't say whether it was accidental or intentional."

"But the force was hard enough to kill her?"

"In my opinion, yes."

Chaz choked back grief. He'd considered telling his parents about the body but hadn't wanted to panic them because they'd all assumed Peyton and Ruth were together. "Thank you, Dr. Sagebrush. I'll talk to my parents and we'll be in touch."

Then they could finally lay Ruth to rest the way she deserved.

Still, as he ended the call, the questions pummeled him again.

He didn't realize Tawny-Lynn had gotten out of bed until she touched his arm. "What's wrong, Chaz?"

His gaze raked over her. She'd pulled on her robe again, but she looked rested, and her lips looked swollen from his kisses. His first instinct was to drag her back to bed and lose himself inside her, to chase away the darkness eating at his soul.

But something shiny sparkled in the sunlight, catching his eye. Something on the floor by the bed...

Realization suddenly hit him and he pushed past Tawny-Lynn, knelt and picked it up. A charm bracelet.

Ruth's charm bracelet.

"Where did you get this?" he asked, his throat so dry he nearly choked on the words.

"Chaz—"

Anger seared him as his gaze met hers. "Where did you get it?"

"Yesterday, outside," she said, her voice cracking.

"By the grave?"

She nodded, her hands digging into her robe. "Chaz, was that the M.E.? Was it Peyton's body?"

"You know what he said." Chaz's voice turned cold. "You found this, you knew it was Ruth in that grave instead of Peyton, didn't you?"

"No...that's not true." Tawny-Lynn shook her head, her face paling.

"Yes, you did." He dangled the bracelet in front of her. "You knew yesterday and you let me believe it was Peyton." His fingers dug into her arms. "Or did you know before that?"

"What? No, of course not."

"Is that what you forgot seven years ago? That Ruth was buried on your ranch?" A muscle tightened in his jaw. "Did you know she was here all along, Tawny-Lynn? Is that why you left town, because you knew and you were lying to everyone?"

"No," she said, although her voice sounded weak, defeated.

"You *did* know. What happened? Did Ruth and Peyton drag you from the crash, then leave?"

"No— I don't know," Tawny-Lynn whispered. "I told you I don't remember. I didn't see the person's face."

"Then why was Ruth buried here? How did she get from the crash to your ranch?"

Tears blurred Tawny-Lynn's eyes. "I have no idea," she murmured.

Chaz struggled to piece together the facts, for some scenario that made sense. "You said Peyton was involved with a married man. Maybe she saw the accident as a way to escape. Or—" his mind took a dangerous leap "—maybe he caused the crash, then Peyton was going to run off with him. Ruth could have tried to stop her and the man… or Peyton…hit Ruth, then buried her here so we wouldn't find her."

"But," Tawny-Lynn said, her eyes filled with denial, "Peyton loved your sister. Peyton would never have hurt Ruth or have left her."

He released her so abruptly she stumbled backward. "Then tell me what happened, dammit!"

"I told you, I don't know. Maybe whoever killed Ruth forced Peyton to go with him."

"Or—" he said between clenched teeth. "Hell,

your father was a drunk. Maybe Ruth came to tell your father that Peyton was running off, and they argued—and he killed her."

"Chaz, you're jumping to conclusions."

Chaz dropped his hands from her, wishing he'd never touched her. "Or Peyton ran away with her lover and left my sister here in the ground."

"How could you believe Peyton would do that?"

"Where is she?" he barked. "Where's she been all these years?"

"I don't know!" Tawny-Lynn cried. "If I did, don't you think I would have told you?"

His stomach was churning, his eyes blurry. He didn't know what to believe anymore. What to think.

Whether he could trust Tawny-Lynn or not.

So he finished dressing, grabbed his gun and holster and headed to the door.

He had to bury his sister and give her the rightful memorial she deserved.

But first he had to tell his parents. And that would be the hardest thing he'd ever done in his life.

TAWNY-LYNN BRUSHED away tears as Chaz stormed out the door. Her heart was breaking.

How could Chaz believe that her sister had killed Ruth? Or that her father had?

He had no reason to hurt Ruth.

But she had no answer for how Ruth's body had come to be buried at White Forks.

Still, she hadn't lied to Chaz....

But he thought she'd covered up for Peyton. If he believed that after the intimacy they'd shared the night before, then everyone else would.

If only she knew who Peyton had been involved with.

She paced the room, racking her brain, then remembered that Chaz had mentioned that Keith Plumbing had been a suspect years ago. He would have been in his early twenties and was nice looking.

What if he and Peyton had been in love?

Maybe her sister had pushed him to leave his wife, and he'd flown into a fit of rage and killed Peyton? Maybe Ruth witnessed the murder, or she'd known about him, and he killed her to keep her quiet, then buried her on White Forks to throw suspicion off himself and onto her father.

They hadn't found Peyton's body on the ranch.

That didn't mean it wasn't there.

Determined to uncover the truth, she quickly showered and dressed, then looked up Keith Plumbing's address. She could confront him at work, but she'd probably get more information if she faced him in person at home.

And his wife... If he'd cheated on her with Peyton, odds were that he'd cheated another time. Maybe more.

Twenty minutes later, she parked at Plumbing's house, an older, brick ranch in a moderate subdivision near town. The community was run-down and needed some landscaping, but most of the houses looked decent with his repair and renovation business. Plumbing probably did odd jobs in his own neighborhood.

She parked in the drive, noting the tricycles in the yard. Apparently the Plumbings had young children.

A MORNING BREEZE stirred, lifting her hair as Tawny-Lynn walked up the steps to the front door. She rang the bell, anxiety plucking at her at the sound of children screeching inside. If she accused Plumbing of an affair and his wife didn't know, she might be tearing apart a marriage.

The door opened, and a woman in her late twenties with bleached-blond hair answered, a baby on one hip, two toddlers holding on to her legs.

"If you're selling something, I'm not interested," the woman said.

Tawny-Lynn caught the door edge before the woman could close it. "I'm not selling anything, Mrs. Plumbing. My name is Tawny-Lynn Boulder. I need to talk to you."

A nervous tick tugged at the corner of the woman's mouth. She patted the towheaded little boy beside her. "Herman, you and Jerry go watch cartoons." The boys raced off, sliding on the floor as if they were skating. Mrs. Plumbing patted the baby's back. "What's this about?"

Tawny-Lynn explained that she'd come back to sell the ranch. "Mrs. Plumbing, I know the police questioned your husband seven years ago when my sister and Ruth Camden first went missing."

"They harassed him, you mean." She hugged the baby tighter to her. "Keith is a good man. A good father."

Tawny-Lynn inhaled. "Since I returned, I learned that my sister was having an affair with a married man before she disappeared. I'm not proud of that, but if it's true, I need to know who it was."

Mrs. Plumbing narrowed her eyes. "You think she was seeing Keith?"

"I don't know," Tawny-Lynn said. "But yesterday we found Ruth Camden's body on my father's ranch. If Peyton had pushed this man to leave his wife, then—"

"You bitch," Mrs. Plumbing snarled. "How dare you come to my house and suggest that my husband slept with your sister. And now you're trying to make out like he killed her and Ruth Camden."

"I'm sorry. I'm just looking for the truth—"

"Well, the truth is that Keith never slept with your sister, and he sure as hell didn't kill anyone." She grabbed the door. "Now get off my property before I make you leave myself."

Tawny-Lynn knotted her hands. "All right. But if I find out you're lying, I'll be back. And next time I'll bring the sheriff with me."

The woman slammed the door in her face.

Tawny-Lynn gritted her teeth and rushed back to the car. She'd certainly made another enemy now.

But Mrs. Plumbing had been defensive and nervous when she'd first realized who she was. Was she lying to cover for her husband?

Chapter Fifteen

Chaz forced his emotions at bay as he delivered the bad news to his parents. His mother was hunched in her favorite armchair, crying quietly, while his father had poured himself a drink, downed it and paced the living room.

"You found her on the White Forks Ranch?"

"Yes," Chaz said. "Actually Tawny-Lynn discovered the grave when she was weeding the flowerbeds."

His father whirled on him, eyes enraged, a vein throbbing in his forehead. "I told you that girl was lying years ago. She probably knew our baby was there all along."

"I can't believe her body was this close all these years." His mother dried her face with a handkerchief. "I always held out hope that somehow she'd survived."

So had he. But she'd been dead all along. Dead while they'd organized search parties, posted fliers, made television appearances to plead for her return.

"Boulder was nothing but a lousy drunk," his father growled. "And Tawny-Lynn covered for him."

Chaz's head ached from trying to sort through the situation. He'd accused Tawny-Lynn of the same thing. But as rational thoughts returned, he couldn't imagine her having hidden such a secret for so long.

Not when the police and town had persecuted her.

She would have broken if she'd known something.

Unless her father had killed Ruth instead of Peyton's lover, and Tawny-Lynn had been afraid of her old man.

But the hurt in her eyes had been too real for her to have lied. Besides, if she'd known the body was there all along, why report it now?

Chaz knelt in front of his mother and cradled her hands between his. "Mom, I promise you, I will get to the bottom of this."

She leaned forward and hugged him, her body trembling with grief. "I don't want to lose you, too, Chaz."

"You won't," he said softly. He glanced at his father who was still pacing, his agitation mounting with every second. Obviously Gerome Camden wasn't calm enough to comfort his wife. The day Ruth had gone missing, something inside his father had died, and he'd never been the same.

The confirmation of her death would probably

change him even more, make him retreat deeper into his shell. "Is there anyone I can call to come and stay with you, Mom? How about your friend LuAnn?"

She nodded and released him, but squeezed his arm. "Yes, honey, LuAnn would be nice."

"All right. Then I'm going to issue a statement to the press. Maybe airing the story again will trigger someone's memory, or prompt a witness to come forward."

Like Peyton's married lover. What did the man know about Ruth's death?

His father paused, the lines around his mouth sagging. "Do you think talking to the press is a good idea?"

"Tawny-Lynn learned that her sister was seeing a married man. If we find him, he might fill in the blanks."

"You think he killed Ruth?" his father asked.

"It's possible. And if he did, he'll pay for it."

"I suppose we'll have to make arrangements," his mother said, another round of tears flooding her eyes.

"I'll let you know when the M.E. releases her," Chaz said.

"When you do that press conference, tell the public we're offering a reward of $50,000 for any information leading to an arrest," his father said. "This time maybe it'll do some good."

Chaz agreed, kissed his mother then called her friend LuAnn as he walked back to his car. LuAnn expressed her regrets and promised to rush over to be with her.

He phoned the mayor, the head of the local paper and the nearest television station along with the FBI agent Justin Thorpe who was spearheading the task force to look into the case of the other missing women. By noon, Chaz stood in front of a podium to address them.

He began by reiterating the details of the original case. "With deep sadness, I'm here today to announce that we have located the body of my sister, Ruth Camden. Her body was found on White Forks Ranch, but at this time we have not located Peyton Boulder. We've recently learned that Peyton may have been having an affair with a married man before the accident and that affair may have played a part in her disappearance. At this point, we do not know the man's identity. If anyone knows the name of this man, or has any information regarding his whereabouts or the death of Ruth Camden, please contact the police. Ruth's parents, Mr. and Mrs. Gerome Camden, are offering a reward of $50,000 for information that leads to an arrest in this case. Thank you for your time."

Several hands flew up and the questions began.

Chaz answered them as best he could, silently praying that unlike years before, this time someone would come forward.

TAWNY-LYNN STARED at the television screen, her heart in her throat. Relaying the news about Ruth's death had to have been difficult for Chaz.

The Camdens probably blamed her, too.

But she no longer cared what they thought. She'd lived with the pain of knowing they'd hated her for years.

But she did care about Chaz.

And she wanted justice for Ruth.

Fresh tears threatened, and she stood, deciding to purge her anxiety, but she couldn't stomach working in the flowerbeds or outdoors.

Not after her earlier discovery.

Although if Peyton were buried on the ranch, surely the search party would have found her grave.

Desperate to block the images from her mind, she resorted to more cleaning, her stomach clenching at the sight of the drawers and cabinets the crime team had rooted through. She washed and dusted and polished walls and floors and furniture until the afternoon bled into evening.

Exhausted, she showered, then poured herself a glass of wine as she fixed a salad, but before she had a chance to drink it, the house phone rang.

She jumped, startled. She'd forgotten to have it disconnected. It was probably a solicitor, but on the off chance it was Chaz or someone calling about Ruth's body, maybe with a tip, she grabbed the handset.

"Hello."

Silence echoed over the line, then she heard the sound of someone breathing.

Anxiety ripped through her. "Who is this?" The person who'd left those bloody messages? The one who'd tried to kill her?

Another heavy breath, and fury shot through Tawny-Lynn. "Listen to me, if you're the person who tried to kill me, I'm not going anywhere until I find out the truth."

Her fingers felt clammy as she tightened her grip on the phone. "Okay, you coward, I'm hanging up—"

"No, don't."

Tawny-Lynn froze, her chest heaving for air. The voice belonged to a woman. But it was muffled. Still it sounded...almost familiar.

"Who is this?" she asked again.

"I...know who your sister was sleeping with."

Was this Keith Plumbing's wife? Maybe she'd changed her mind and decided to come forward.

"Tell me his name."

"Not over the phone," the woman whispered. "Meet me at the park at the creek and I'll tell you everything."

"What do you mean 'everything'?"

The line went dead before the caller replied.

Tawny-Lynn sat for a moment, contemplating what to do as the wind rattled the windowpanes of the old house. If the caller had been Plumbing's wife, then why didn't she identify herself?

Maybe her husband had been in the house.

But why the clandestine meeting?

Could it be a setup? Someone working with the man who'd tried to kill her?

Or…what if the person who'd killed Ruth was a woman? Maybe the wife of the man Peyton had been sleeping with? She could have killed Peyton and then Ruth.

And now she wanted her dead.

She picked up the phone to call Chaz, but hesitated, her heart aching as she remembered the accusations he'd hurled at her.

No, she'd go alone.

But she grabbed the rifle to carry with her just in case she was walking into a trap.

CHAZ MET WITH the Texas Ranger and Sheriff Blair from Sunset Mesa after the press conference, then spent the afternoon fending off calls, hoping to get some valid tips.

But as dusk fell, nothing had come through.

The front door of the sheriff's office burst open, and Keith Plumbing stalked in, his face blazing with anger. He yanked off his work hat, then propped his hands on Chaz's desk.

"How dare you send Tawny-Lynn Boulder over to question my wife, and make accusations against me?"

"What?" Chaz forced his voice to remain calm. "I didn't send Tawny-Lynn to do anything."

Plumbing lifted his hands from the desk and folded his arms. "Then why the hell did she go to my house and ask my wife if I was running around with her sister?"

Chaz blew out an exasperated breath. "I guess because she wants answers." He stood, towering over Plumbing by at least a foot. "Did you have an affair with Peyton?"

"You've got to be kidding me!" Plumbing cursed. "I can't believe this crap. I didn't deserve the law coming down on me seven years ago, and I sure as hell don't now."

"You didn't answer the question," Chaz said calmly. "Did you sleep with Peyton Boulder?"

"No," Plumbing shouted. "For God's sake, she was a teenager back then. I'm not stupid."

Chaz simply stared him down. "Then why did the sheriff question you?"

"Because I was in the wrong place at the wrong time," Plumbing said. "My wife and I'd only been married a couple of years and were having money trouble. Then she gets pregnant on top of that, and I blew one out at a bar one night. Wound up in a bar brawl and got arrested. Once you get in the system, you're an easy patsy."

"Maybe," Chaz said, wondering if Plumbing simply had a chip on his shoulder or if he was lying to cover his butt. "But maybe you deserved to get looked at."

The man shot him a seething look. "Listen, Sheriff, I learned my lesson. I've been clean for seven years, go home to my wife every night. I didn't sleep with Peyton, and I sure as hell didn't kill your sister. So tell Tawny-Lynn that if she keeps harassing me, I'm going to get a lawyer and sue her six ways till Sunday."

Plumbing rattled the chair with his hands as he turned and stalked out the door. Maybe the man had control of his drinking, but he wasn't sure about his temper.

Chaz had to put aside his feelings toward Tawny-Lynn, jumbled as they were, and make sure she was safe. He'd also better pass on Plumbing's warning and tell her to let him do the police work.

He grabbed his Stetson and keys and headed out to his squad car. Plumbing's truck was already disappearing out of sight, headed in the same direction as White Forks.

Chaz turned from the parking lot and followed, riding Plumbing until the man made the turn toward his own subdivision. Relieved Plumbing hadn't planned to pay Tawny-Lynn a visit in the mood he was in, Chaz sped toward the ranch. But just as he neared the mile-long drive, Tawny-Lynn barreled from the ranch, cut a right and drove away from town.

Curious, Chaz followed behind her, maintaining enough distance not to spook her, but staying close enough that if someone else was following her, he'd be able to detect it.

Two miles down the flat country road, she veered onto the graveled road leading to the creek park. The place used to be a popular teen make-out spot, but he thought they'd found a new location for their rendezvous. Although it was dark and deserted, he'd discovered dopers out here twice. Last month he'd even broken up a deal going down.

He made a mental note to have the city fix the streetlights as half of them were burned out. The playground needed reworking, as well. No wonder the residents didn't use the park much anymore.

He spotted Tawny-Lynn driving to the section where the picnic tables were located and he flipped off his lights, not wanting to alert her he was following.

She veered into a spot in the parking lot, then sat for a few minutes, and he did the same, making sure he was hidden by a cluster of trees. Finally another car rolled up, a small sedan that slowed as it neared Tawny-Lynn's car.

She must be meeting someone. But why the hell would she agree to meet someone out here in the dark where it was deserted?

He thought she had more sense than that.

Protective instincts rushed to life, and he checked his gun, then watched as a woman clad in all black clothing with a hoodie climbed from the sedan.

Tawny-Lynn's truck door opened, and she stepped out. A breath of relief escaped him when he saw her swing the shotgun up beside her.

He opened his door, careful to close it without making a sound, then slowly eased his way along the creek edge until he was hidden behind a tree near the park bench. The woman in the hoodie gestured toward the bench, then Tawny-Lynn dropped the rifle to her side and followed.

He tilted his head, waiting on the woman to step into the moonlight so he could see her face.

When she finally did, his heart stopped. It couldn't be…

Chapter Sixteen

Tawny-Lynn stared at the woman in front of her in shock. It wasn't possible…was it?

"Hello, sis," the woman said.

Tawny-Lynn shook her head in denial. She'd expected Mrs. Plumbing, but never Peyton.

But it *was* her.

Her hair had darkened, streaked with red now, unnatural as if she'd dyed it. But she lowered the hood and those same blue eyes looked back at her. Blue eyes she'd looked into so many times.

She had to swallow twice to make her voice work. "You're alive. What? How?"

"I'm sorry, Tawny-Lynn," Peyton whispered. "Sorry I left you to deal with everything, but I was scared."

Relief mingled with stunned surprise, but anger followed, nearly choking her. "You let me think you were missing, kidnapped, maybe raped or murdered…." Fresh tears made her voice turn to gravel. "How could you do that to me?"

"I can explain," Peyton said. "But please put away Dad's rifle."

Tawny-Lynn had forgotten about the gun. "I thought you might be the person whose been trying to kill me."

"What?" Peyton gasped. "Oh, my God, I— Why would someone try to kill you?"

Tawny-Lynn laid the rifle on the table with a huff. "Because they think I know something about the accident. Everyone in town thinks I've covered up for whoever took you and Ruth." Her voice rose an octave. "But you've been alive all this time and Ruth was dead and buried on our ranch."

"I...didn't know about Ruth," Peyton cried. "I... thought she'd run off, too."

Tawny-Lynn massaged her temples where a headache pulsed. She had missed her sister so much, had wanted to see her again, had prayed she was alive so many times.

And now here she was, and she didn't how to react.

Tawny-Lynn sank down at the picnic table, numb. Peyton followed her, then sat down next to her, and pulled her sister in close.

"I'm so sorry, honey, really, I...wanted to call you. To come back. To explain."

"But you didn't," Tawny-Lynn said in a pained whisper. Still, she didn't fight her when Peyton wrapped her arms around her.

"I was a coward," Peyton said against her ear. "And a terrible sister. But...I had my reasons."

A noise sounded nearby, gravel and twigs snapped, then a harsh male voice echoed in the wind.

"So you did lie, Tawny-Lynn. No wonder you went away. Have you been living with Peyton all this time?"

Tawny-Lynn pulled away from Peyton and glanced up, her heart racing. Chaz glared at the two of them with rage in his eyes.

"No...that's not true," she said in a hoarse whisper.

"Then what is the truth?" Chaz said coldly. "Because I sure as hell don't know anymore."

Tawny-Lynn's head was swimming. "I don't know," she said, "but I didn't lie to you."

"Yet here you are with your long-lost sister."

Memories of the night in Chaz's arms seemed so distant that she ached to turn back the clock. But too much had happened.

Whatever closeness they'd shared had dissipated in the light of day. And if Chaz believed that she'd lied and covered up his sister's murder, then he didn't know her at all.

And he certainly could never love her.

CHAZ REACHED FOR his handcuffs. He wanted to haul both Tawny-Lynn and her sister in for lying, for leading the police on a wild-goose chase for Peyton when for all he knew she'd killed Ruth and left her at White Forks.

"None of this is Tawny-Lynn's fault." Peyton shot up from the bench like a protective big sister. Only where had she been when the town and their father had persecuted Tawny-Lynn?

She couldn't have known where Peyton was back then. She'd been too traumatized and had that head injury. And her reaction when his family and the town had turned on her had been too real.

"Did you kill my sister, Peyton?" he asked.

Peyton's eyes widened. "No! Heavens no, Chaz. I loved Ruth." She crossed her arms and shifted onto the balls of her feet, the ground crunching beneath her shoes. "In fact, I didn't know Ruth was dead until I saw your press conference earlier. That's when I called Tawny-Lynn to meet me."

His gaze shot to Tawny-Lynn's, but she was watching her sister with a mixture of awe and hurt. "Where have you been?" Tawny-Lynn whispered.

Peyton cleared her throat. "In Tennessee," she said softly. "I...had to leave town. I didn't know what else to do."

"You could have come home," Tawny-Lynn said. "The entire town was looking for you. I was looking for you. And Dad..."

"Dad and I weren't getting along back then," Peyton said. "That's one reason I left."

"You were having an affair with a married man," Chaz said sharply.

Peyton's eyes widened. "How do you know about that?"

"I talked to J.J. and Cindy and Rudy," Tawny-Lynn said.

Peyton's face paled in the dim moonlight. "What else did they tell you?"

"Nothing," Tawny-Lynn said. "So who was he? Did you run off with him?"

"No." A shudder ripped up Peyton's body making her look scared and vulnerable. "But he is the reason I left."

"And what about Ruth?" Chaz asked. "Did you two fight about him, then you killed her to keep her quiet?"

Peyton shook her head fiercely. "I told you, Chaz, I would never have hurt Ruth."

"But you did argue about him," Tawny-Lynn said. "You were arguing and whispering on the bus."

"You heard us?" Peyton asked.

"I didn't understand what you were saying, but I knew you were upset. Then someone ran into the bus and the driver lost control, and we crashed into the ravine."

Peyton tucked a strand of Tawny-Lynn's hair behind her ear. "Yes, and when I came to, I smelled smoke. You were hurt, sis, and I pulled you out before the bus exploded."

"What about Ruth?" Chaz asked.

"She was gone," Peyton said. "I...looked around and couldn't find her."

"What do you mean, you couldn't find her?"

"She wasn't in the bus," Peyton cried. "You have to believe me, Chaz. If she had been, I would have saved her, too."

"How could she have been gone?" Tawny-Lynn asked.

Peyton shrugged, her expression tormented. "I don't know. At first I thought that maybe he... That she left with him. I was scared so I ran and hitched a ride with a trucker. That's how I wound up in Tennessee."

Chaz gritted his teeth. "Who did you think she ran off with?"

"You have to understand, we were young. I was petrified," Peyton said.

"You didn't answer my question," Chaz barked.

Peyton gave Tawny-Lynn a pleading look. "Tell us what happened, Peyton. Ever since I came back, someone's been threatening me. A man even broke into the ranch and tried to strangle me."

"I'm so sorry. I thought when I left it would be over."

"It's not over until we lock him up," Tawny-Lynn said.

Peyton sank back on the park bench, twisting her hands together. "I can't believe he actually killed Ruth. He was married, and when he broke it off with me, I was devastated. I was stupid and thought I was in love with him."

"You wanted to marry him?" Tawny-Lynn asked gently.

"Yes, then he started hitting on Ruth, pressuring her to have sex with him."

Chaz's pulse pounded.

"I realized then that he'd used me. That I wasn't the only one, so I told Ruth to stay away from him. That if he harassed her, she should tell her folks." She looked up at Chaz. "That's what we argued about. She didn't want to tell them. But he threatened us and…that's why I ran."

Tawny-Lynn took her sister's hands in hers. "Who was it, Peyton? You have to tell us his name so we can make this right."

Peyton nodded, although her voice quivered when she spoke. "It was Coach Wake."

ANOTHER SHOCK WAVE rolled through Tawny-Lynn at Peyton's words. Coach Wake had seduced Peyton? Had hit on the other girls?

"Our softball coach?" Tawny-Lynn asked. "He slept with you?"

Peyton dropped her head as if ashamed. "He seduced me, and I fell for him like a fool. But then he went after Ruth, and I heard other girls talking about how he'd done the same to them. That he'd come on to them in the locker room. I had to stop him from bothering Ruth. So after the game that day, I told him we were going to go to your parents."

"That's when he threatened you?" Chaz asked.

Peyton nodded. "He said he'd ruin both our lives if we told anyone." She gave Chaz a pleading look. "Ruth was terrified of your parents finding out. She didn't want to embarrass your father and begged me to keep quiet."

"Then you dragged Peyton out. Where was Ruth?" Chaz asked.

"I don't know."

"You should have stuck around and told someone. Then my sister might still be alive."

"I know, but I was terrified. The coach was so mad when I talked to him after the game that he followed the bus. He's the one who caused us to crash."

Tawny-Lynn recognized guilt in her sister's eyes and knew that she blamed herself.

"I should arrest you for not coming forward," Chaz said. "For covering up for a murderer."

Tawny-Lynn's protective instincts surged to life. "Listen, Chaz, Peyton told you the truth. She didn't hurt Ruth, she tried to save her. And she ran because she was scared, not to cover for the coach."

"Your sister was the best friend I ever had," Peyton said earnestly. "If you arrest the coach, I'll testify about the sexual harassment and that he hit the bus."

"Sexual harassment?" Chaz muttered. "That's

only the beginning of the charges I'm going to bring against the monster. On top of sexual assault, I'm charging him with five counts of murder."

Tawny-Lynn realized he was right. If Coach Wake had caused the crash, he'd killed three of her teammates, and the bus driver.

And now it appeared that he'd killed Ruth.

Had he tried to kill her because he thought she knew about his affair with Peyton? Or was he afraid she'd remember that he caused those four deaths?

CHAZ STUDIED PEYTON for a moment before he left. "Can I trust you not to leave town?

"Yes." Peyton curved her arm around Tawny-Lynn. "I was seventeen and scared back then, Chaz. I'm not a kid anymore. I want to make up for the past. And I'm not going to allow Ruth's killer to get away."

"We'll go back to the ranch together," Tawny-Lynn said.

Peyton rose and took Chaz's hand. "I promise you that I won't run again. It's time Coach Wake got what he deserves." Regret lined her face. "Besides, I feel terrible that I didn't come forward seven years ago. No matter how many young girls he's pressured into having sex with him since then."

Rage heated Chaz's blood at the thought. She was right.

"You two go back to the ranch. I'll let you know when he's in custody."

Tawny-Lynn nodded, and he waited until they got in their cars and left for White Forks, then he strode back to his squad car. He replayed images of Coach Wake in his head. He was always friendly, outgoing, a real charmer with the moms.

Because he was taking advantage of their daughters behind their backs. Pressuring them into sex, then threatening them so they wouldn't reveal his dirty little secret.

A secret he'd killed for to keep quiet.

Chaz started the engine and peeled from the park. He checked his watch for the time and realized the coach should be home from school by now. That is, unless they had a game.

His body teemed with anger as he drove straight to Wake's house, a nice two-story in a new development close to town. The yard was well kept, the flowerbeds filled with flowers, the house freshly painted.

Everything that shouted that Coach Wake was a nice, family man.

Now Chaz knew differently.

He checked to make sure his weapon was secure, his handcuffs intact, then walked up to the front door and rang the bell. A few moments later, the man's wife, Susan, answered the door. She was pretty with brown hair and green eyes. And she was very pregnant.

"Sheriff, what can I do for you?"

"Is your husband home?"

She propped her hip against the door frame. "No, they had a game."

"Away or home?"

"Home."

Sympathy for the woman in front of him clawed at him. But then again, what if she'd known about the sex with the young girls?

Either way, if he told her his plans to arrest her husband, she might warn him and he'd probably run.

He didn't intend for the creep to get away.

"All right, I'll catch up with him later."

She cleared her throat. "Can I tell him the reason you stopped by?"

"No, thanks," he said. "I just need to talk to him, that's all."

He walked away as if the conversation could wait, but the town had already waited seven years for justice, and he refused to hold off another day.

He climbed back in the squad car and drove to the high school, parked and headed to the bleachers. The stands on both sides were filled with parents, teens and kids. The game was in the last inning, the score tied.

Memories of watching Ruth, Peyton and Tawny-Lynn play haunted him. If he'd known back then what Coach Wake was up to, he would have stood up for the girls, especially his sister.

Why hadn't she come to him?

Maybe she'd planned to. But the coach had killed her first.

One of the girls hit a ground ball and the other team's player missed it, allowing the Camden Cats to score the winning run.

Cheers erupted taking him back to that fatal day when Tawny-Lynn had won the game for the team.

And everything else had been lost.

The team raced onto the field, cheering and shouting and hugging each other. The coach was beaming, high-fiving the girls, as he joined the players to celebrate.

The handcuffs jangled at Chaz's hip as he strode onto the field. The other team was heading to their bus, but family members and friends of the Cats stood shouting and clapping in the stands.

Coach Wake's face went ashen when Chaz reached for the cuffs, as if he knew the past had finally caught up with him.

"You're under arrest, Coach Wake." Chaz jerked the man's arms behind him. The girls on the team paused in their celebrations, shocked. The stands grew quiet, curious whispers rumbling through the crowd.

"You don't have to do this in front of everyone," Coach Wake growled.

Chaz snapped the handcuffs into place.

"Yes, I do. You should be grateful I don't shout the charges over the intercom." He knew arresting

Wake in front of the team and town might be considered cold.

But he didn't give a damn.

It was only fitting that the residents see the man who'd torn their town apart handcuffed and hauled to jail.

Chapter Seventeen

"Where exactly did you find Ruth's body?" Peyton asked as they parked at the ranch.

Tawny-Lynn led her sister to the side of the house. "There. I was weeding the flowerbeds and found her bracelet. Then…the body."

Peyton studied it with a solemn face. "I don't understand how she ended up here. This is miles from the site of the crash."

"I don't understand, either," Tawny-Lynn said. "Unless the coach took her from the site, killed her then decided to hide her body here in case someone discovered her."

Peyton nodded, although she looked unconvinced. Shadows plagued her eyes as she turned toward Tawny-Lynn. "I'm so sorry I left you to deal with everything. I—that's the one thing I regret most."

"I was so scared," Tawny-Lynn admitted. "Every time I thought about what might be happening to you—"

Peyton drew her into a hug. "I'm so sorry I put

you through that. I never meant to hurt you or Dad. I just didn't know what to do."

Tawny-Lynn wanted to forgive her sister with no questions asked, but she had suffered for years and she needed answers.

"Come on inside. I want to hear where you went, what happened after you left."

They hooked arms together and walked around to the front porch. Tawny-Lynn remembered the bloody deer and threats and made herself glance around the house and yard in case her attacker had returned.

But hopefully Coach Wake was locked up so they were safe.

She unlocked the door but Peyton hesitated in the doorway. "I don't feel like I belong here," she said in a haunted whisper.

Tawny-Lynn squeezed her hand. "Neither do I. You should have seen the place when I came back. Dad's drinking was really bad the past few years, and he'd turned into a hoarder. There wasn't an inch of clean, empty space anywhere."

Peyton walked into the den and stood by the fireplace. "I…should have let him know I was alive before he died."

Tawny-Lynn simply looked at her sister, unable to let her off the hook. Peyton's disappearance had sent her father over the edge and drastically changed all their lives.

Knowing they both needed something to dispel

the tension, she went to the kitchen, opened a bottle of wine and brought them both a glass.

Peyton cradled it in her trembling hands. "Thanks."

Tawny-Lynn sipped hers, needing liquid courage. "Dad took your disappearance hard. He...blamed me."

"You?" Peyton sank down onto the hearth. "Why? You were injured."

"Didn't you read the papers or watch the news?" she asked, a trace of bitterness in her voice.

Peyton shook her head. "Not at first. I was... confused. Terrified and alone, trying to figure out where to go and what to do."

Tawny-Lynn swallowed hard. "I had a concussion from the accident, and my memories were all scrambled. I knew someone rescued me from the bus, but I couldn't see a face. The parents of the other girls, Chaz's parents, even Dad blamed me. They thought if I could remember, they'd be able to find you and Ruth."

"Oh, Tawny-Lynn." Peyton stared into her red wine. "I never thought about that. I...guess I didn't think at all. I felt so stupid to have slept with the coach, especially when I realized he hit on other girls."

"You and Dad argued a lot those last three months. Did he know about Coach?"

Peyton shook her head. "He caught me sneaking back in one night, and accused me of being a slut. We got into a terrible fight.... But he was right."

Tawny-Lynn softened. "You weren't a slut, Peyton, just a vulnerable girl. Coach Wake took advantage of that."

Regret flickered in Peyton's eyes. "But I should have come forward and spoken up. No telling how many girls he's done the same thing to since."

She was right. Seven years—seven *teams* of girls...

"Well, you're here now, and Chaz has gone to arrest Coach Wake so he can't hurt anyone else."

Peyton swirled her wine in her glass. "But it won't bring back Ruth."

She sat down beside her sister, soaking in the fact that she was alive. "No, it won't. But she'll finally get the justice she deserves. Then all of us can move on."

CHAZ PHONED HIS parents on the way to the jail and asked them to meet him at his office. He didn't want them to learn the news about the coach's arrest from the gossip mill. They deserved to hear it from him, and to face the man who'd killed Ruth.

Coach Wake sat with his head down, his jaw set as Chaz parked. He walked around the car, opened the door and hauled him out, keeping a firm grip on the man's arm as he escorted him inside.

His deputy's eyebrows shot up, but he watched silently as Chaz fingerprinted Wake and booked him.

"I don't know what the hell you think you're

doing, Sheriff, but you've made a huge mistake," Coach Wake snapped.

"You've harassed your last girl," Chaz said through clenched teeth.

"Where did you dig up these phony charges? None of the girls on my team would say anything bad about me."

Chaz shoved his face into the coach's. "And why is that? Because you threaten to destroy their lives if they talk." It wasn't a question, but a statement.

The coach stiffened. "I would never threaten one of those kids."

"I have a witness who says differently."

A seed of panic flared in Wake's eyes. "Who are you talking about?"

"All in due time." He grabbed the man by his arm and hauled him through the double doors to the back.

"You're going to be sorry for this," Coach Wake said angrily as Chaz threw him into a cell.

Chaz slammed the cell door shut and jangled the keys. "I don't think so. You're finally going to pay for what you've done."

"I want a lawyer!" Wake shouted. "Give me my phone call now."

"You'll get it," Chaz said as he headed back to the front. He needed time to compose himself before he interrogated the man, needed to have evidence compiled and to build his case. He would need a formal statement by Peyton, as well.

In the front office, he paused to explain the situation to his deputy. "Send those prints over to the lab," Chaz said. "Tell them to compare them to the prints found at the Boulder place and any they might have found on my sister's bracelet."

Seconds later, his parents stormed in the door, looking haggard. "What's going on, Chaz?" his mother cried.

His father's expression bordered on irate. "You arrested Ruth's killer?"

Chaz nodded. "I did make an arrest, but I need to explain some things to both of you before word gets out."

His mother clenched his arm. "What things?"

"Did you or did you not arrest Ruth's killer?" his father bellowed.

"Just come in my office and sit down." He led them to his private office and offered them coffee, but they both declined.

"Just tell us what's going on," his father demanded.

Chaz crossed his arms and began by explaining that Peyton Boulder was alive.

His mother gasped. "What? Where's she been all this time?"

His father gave him a scathing look. "Did she kill Ruth?"

Chaz shook his head. "No, I believe Coach Wake did, but I need time to build a case. I have motive, though."

His mother paled. "What motive?"

Chaz pulled up a chair and faced her, noting that his father was still standing, his body ramrod straight as if bracing himself for more bad news.

"Peyton claims that Coach Wake seduced her, that she had an affair with him, then he hit on Ruth."

His mother's eyes widened in shock. "No…."

Chaz nodded. "When Ruth told Peyton, Peyton realized that the coach was sexually harassing other girls. After the game that day, Ruth threatened to come to you two and tell you about it, but the coach warned her that she'd be sorry if she did."

"He threatened her?" his mother asked.

"That son of a bitch," his father muttered. "Where is he? I'm going to kill him."

Chaz blocked his father from exiting his office. "No, Dad, you aren't going to do anything. You're going to let me handle this. He's in custody now."

"What did he do to our little girl?" his mother whispered.

Chaz stood his ground against his father when he tried to push past him. "Peyton said he chased the bus down and hit them. Coach Wake is the one who caused the accident that killed those other three girls and the bus driver."

His mother dropped her head into her hands. "Oh, my God…."

"Then he dragged Ruth away and killed her," his father said. "He deserves to die for what he did."

Yes, he did. But first Chaz had to make a solid case. "Now, I want you two to go home. Don't talk to anyone about this. I need Peyton to make a formal statement, then I have to gather as much evidence as possible to make sure Coach Wake doesn't walk."

"If he walks, he won't live long," his father muttered.

"Dad, I understand how you feel, but don't go around saying that to anyone else."

Although his father was right. If Wake walked, the town would probably form a lynch mob and hang him themselves.

TAWNY-LYNN FINALLY put together her famous enchiladas for dinner.

"This is delicious, sis," Peyton said. "You've turned into a good cook."

Tawny-Lynn shrugged, wondering if Chaz would think so. "Cooking is like gardening, it's relaxing to me."

"I can't believe how rundown the ranch looks," Peyton said.

"There's still a lot to do. The weatherman predicted rain the next couple of days. That's why I was working outside, weeding the flowerbeds. Spiffing up the landscaping should help attract a buyer. Although the house needs repairs and my finances are low."

Peyton poured them both more wine. "Did you ever consider moving in and staying here yourself?"

Chaz's face flashed in her mind, and her heart tugged. But any love between them had been one-sided. "No. There's nothing for me in Camden Crossing except bitter memories of how much the town hated me after the accident."

Remorse darkened Peyton's eyes. "That's my fault. And I'll make sure everyone knows it."

Tawny-Lynn sighed. "I'm not sure how everyone will react, Peyton. They may be angry that you didn't come forward sooner."

Peyton's expression turned determined. "I know, but it's time the truth came out. The lies ate at me over the years. And I missed you." Peyton blinked back tears. "When I heard that Ruth's body was found, I realized I couldn't live with myself if I didn't come forward."

They ate in silence for a few moments before Peyton spoke. "Where did you go when you left the ranch?"

Tawny-Lynn bit into her enchilada. "I got a partial scholarship at Texas A&M. The money wasn't enough though, so I took a part-time job at a local lawn-and-garden shop. I guess I'd felt so depressed, dead for so long, that I discovered I liked growing things, watching them come to life. So I majored in landscape architecture."

"You're amazing," Peyton said.

Tawny-Lynn chuckled. "Not really. I started my own business last year, but it's been tough going. When Dad died, I figured I could sell the ranch and put the money into my business."

"You can still do that," Peyton said.

Tawny-Lynn set down her fork. "The ranch belongs to both of us."

Peyton shook her head. "I don't deserve it, not after I let you and Dad down."

"You were a victim," Tawny-Lynn said. "Now let's clean up the dishes, and I want you to tell me where you've been, what you've been doing all this time."

They lapsed back into silence as they cleaned the kitchen, then they retreated to the den in front of the fireplace.

"Now tell me about you," Tawny-Lynn said. "Where have you been living? Did you finish school?"

Peyton curled on the sofa. "I hitched a ride across the country, then wound up staying on the streets for a few weeks."

The images that flashed in Tawny-Lynn's mind terrified her.

"I was scared," Peyton admitted. "Then I met this girl who took me to a group home for teens. She showed me how to make a fake ID and how to get by. I got a job washing dishes at a little diner, then one of the waitresses took a liking to me and invited me to live with her while I earned my GED."

"What did you tell her about your family?"

Heat flooded Peyton's cheeks. "That my mother was dead and that my father was a mean drunk— that I had to run away."

She'd told the partial truth. "What happened then?"

"I lived with her almost five years, then she passed away. But during the time she was alive, she encouraged me to attend a technical school. I became a paralegal and have a decent job."

"It sounds like you did okay."

"I managed, but I was lonely," Peyton admitted softly. "I never stopped missing you and Ruth and wanting to see you." A small smile tugged at her lips. "But I did meet a man through work, and last year we moved in together."

Tawny-Lynn thought about Chaz again and her heart ached. "Maybe I could meet him sometime."

"I'd like that," Peyton said softly.

Tawny-Lynn's cell phone buzzed, and she snatched it up. "Hello."

"I arrested Coach Wake," Chaz said. "Is Peyton still with you?"

"Yes, she's right here."

"Tell her that I need her to come in and sign a formal statement in the morning." His voice sounded terse.

"Okay, we'll be there first thing."

"Thanks." He hung up without another word, and Tawny-Lynn felt bereft. But she pasted on a brave face for her sister. "That was Chaz. He arrested Coach Wake and wants us to come to his office in the morning to sign a statement."

Peyton's hand trembled as she set down her glass. "Tomorrow the town is going to go into shock."

For the second time in seven years. "At least this time, they'll have answers."

Peyton yawned. "I'm going to call Ben in a minute to tell him what's going on."

"Does he know about me? About what happened?" She paused. "About Coach Wake?"

Peyton nodded. "I told him the night before I left to come here. When I heard about Ruth, I broke down. He…was amazing, so supportive."

"I'm glad," Tawny-Lynn said. Maybe there was a happily ever after for one of them in the cards.

HE WATCHED THE ranch from a distance, his nerves on edge. Coach Wake had been arrested. He'd caused the crash that had killed three girls and the bus driver.

And he had killed Ruth.

Soon everyone would know that. Or at least they would *believe* it.

Then *he* would be in the clear.

Unless…Tawny-Lynn remembered his face. That he'd been there that day.

Damn her and her sister, Peyton. All these years he'd wondered where in the hell she was. Why she hadn't come forward.

234 Cold Case at Camden Crossing

It was all her fault. She'd seduced that coach and made him want the other young girls on the team. How many had he taken advantage of?

The man deserved to die. But if he went to jail for four counts of murder, at least he'd rot in jail without parole.

But Tawny-Lynn... She was a problem. She had seen his face today.

One day she still might remember....

It was time he got rid of her for good.

Chapter Eighteen

After his parents left, Chaz decided to question Coach Wake. He wanted his gut reaction before the lawyer showed up and stalled the case with legalities.

Chaz strode back to the cell and found the coach sitting on the bare cot with his head in his hands.

"Talk to me, Coach."

Coach Wake shot him an angry look. "You made a mistake. I never hurt any of those girls."

"Really?" Chaz folded his arms. "Because I have a witness who claims that you pressured her to have sex. That she wasn't the only teenager or girl on the team that you slept with."

"I love my wife," Coach Wake said. "And I love coaching. I can't help it if some impressionable student has a crush on me. It happens to coaches all the time. Doesn't mean I did anything about it."

"This girl has no reason to lie," Chaz said.

"If that's true, then tell me who she is."

Chaz shook his head. "Not yet. But I wanted to

give you the opportunity to do the right thing and confess before things get dirty."

"They will get dirty because I intend to sue you for false arrest and defamation of character."

Chaz grunted, his hands tightening around the bars of the cell. He wanted to choke the truth out of the bastard. "When I finish with you, you'll be begging me for a deal. You killed my sister and you're going to pay for it."

"I didn't kill Ruth," he shouted. "She got out of that bus alive."

"Then you *were* following the bus and caused it to crash."

"That's not what I said."

"I know for a fact that you tried to pressure her into having sex, and that when she threatened to tell my parents, you chased down that bus, ran into it and forced it over the ravine."

Panic streaked the coach's face. "That damn Tawny-Lynn. That's what she told you? Did she finally remember something?"

The quiver in his voice confirmed his guilt in Chaz's mind. "So you admit to being there. But you didn't do anything to save those girls, did you? You left them there to die."

The coach scrubbed a hand over his face, stood and paced the cell. "I'm not admitting anything."

"And when Tawny-Lynn came back, you got worried so you tried to kill her."

Wake clammed up. "I want my lawyer."

Chaz simply glared at him. "Fine. But you are going to jail, Coach. And tomorrow everyone in town is going to know what you did to their children."

"I'm innocent," Coach Wake protested.

Chaz simply turned and left the man to stew in the cell. It would be the first of many nights he'd sleep alone on a cold cot. Maybe one day he'd even feel remorse for what he'd done. Although he didn't appear to feel anything now except the need to protect himself.

But for the first time in years, especially the last two weeks since Tawny-Lynn had returned to Camden Crossing, Chaz allowed himself to relax when he got home.

Even though they'd found out Ruth was dead, they had closure in the arrest of Coach Wake. They knew what had happened to Peyton.

And Tawny-Lynn was safe.

Maybe she'd even decide to stay at White Forks.

He paused as he set the take-out meal he'd picked up at the diner on his table, wondering where that thought had come from. He'd known all along that Tawny-Lynn was here to put White Forks on the market, and that there was no love lost between her and the town.

Hell, some of the townsfolk would probably be furious at Peyton for staying away and leaving them in the dark for so long.

He opened up the foam box and inhaled the

savory scent of homemade meat loaf and mashed potatoes and gravy. His mouth watered. He tried to recall what he'd had for lunch, then remembered he hadn't eaten.

No wonder he was ravenous.

He'd deal with the fallout from the arrest and Peyton's arrival in town tomorrow. His deputy was staying at the jail, watching over their prisoner.

Tonight he was going to steal some much-needed sleep.

He wolfed down the food and chased it with a cold beer, then walked to his office nook and studied the photographs on the wall.

Wake would probably have a lawyer and bail in the next twenty-four hours. Unless Chaz could convince the judge to remand him until his trial.

He phoned his contact at the paper and TV station and requested another press conference. As soon as he had Peyton's official statement in the morning, he'd announce the news of Wake's arrest.

The parents of the dead teens would be riled at the coach, and it would no doubt be an emotional day, but at least now they would have justice.

When his parents finally buried Ruth in the graveyard at their church, her killer would be rotting in jail. And if Wake had pressured other girls to sleep with him, maybe once Peyton went public, the others would, too.

Then he'd make sure Coach Wake never hurt anyone else.

THE BUS WAS ON FIRE. Flames burst through the air, eating at the ceiling and seats. Smoke clogged Tawny-Lynn's lungs as she opened her eyes.

Someone had dragged her from the bus. Her sister. Peyton was alive.

She struggled to sit up, but pain throbbed through every cell in her body. Her leg hurt the most. Then she looked down and saw that it was twisted at an odd angle.

Broken.

"Peyton!" She tried to scream over the noise of the exploding glass as the bus blew, but her voice came out a hoarse whisper.

Where was Peyton?

She blinked, but smoke clogged her vision. Then she saw him...a man...dragging Ruth away.

Panic bubbled inside her. She tried to see the man's face, but he was too far away. Then he turned and looked at her, and she cried out....

His face was blank. An empty black hole....

Tawny-Lynn startled awake and sat up in bed, her pulse clamoring as she looked around the room. It was empty. No one inside.

Only the man from her nightmares. She felt his evil permeating her. Felt his eyes boring into her.

She clenched the sheets, desperately forcing the image back into her head.

A man dragging Ruth away. He wore a dark coat....something gold glinted in the darkness. A ring of some kind?

Or had she imagined it? Maybe it had been embers sparking from the flames.

Was the man Coach Wake? Had she blocked out his face because she'd been too shocked to see him hauling Ruth away?

CHAZ'S CELL PHONE trilled, jarring him from sleep at 6:00 a.m. He reached for it as he climbed from bed and walked to the kitchen to make coffee.

"Sheriff, you'd better get down here now."

Chaz blinked. "What's going on?"

"The parents of the three girls who died in the crash are here along with your father. I swear, we've got a lynch mob on our hands."

Chaz cursed. He should have foreseen that his father would call the other parents.

"I'm on my way." He ended the call, rushed to the bathroom and splashed water on his face, then hurriedly dressed. He picked up coffee on the way, knowing he needed a clear head, and to calm down, because he felt like throwing his father in jail for stirring up trouble.

By the time he arrived, Coach Wake's wife and Alvin Lambert, Wake's attorney, had joined the scene. His deputy stood by the door leading to the back of the jail with his hand at his gun. Lambert had strategically pushed Mrs. Wake to the opposite side and was guarding her as if he expected the parents to physically assault her.

"No one sees Wake until the sheriff says so," his deputy said as Chaz entered.

Chaz's father stood to the right of the other parents, calmer today, although his eyes were livid, revenge flaring in their depths.

Chaz shot him a scathing look. He'd deal with him later.

"Is it true?" Mrs. Pullman asked, her face tormented.

"Coach Wake forced girls to have sex then killed our children!" Mr. Marx shouted.

"Did he?" Mrs. Truman cried.

Chaz held up a hand to calm them. "Listen to me, and listen good. I did make an arrest, but I need time to gather evidence and interrogate Coach Wake."

"If he killed our daughters, you can't let him go free," Mr. Truman said sharply.

"Please, Sheriff," Mrs. Pullman whispered. "We've waited all this time for the truth."

"Trust me, I know how you feel. We all want justice." Chaz cleared his throat to stop another onslaught of questions. "But you have to leave now and let me do my job."

"Sheriff," Lambert cut in. "I need to speak to my client."

"Why are you doing this to my husband?" Mrs. Wake cried. "He's a good man. He would never hurt one of his students."

The door opened and Peyton and Tawny-Lynn

walked in. Shadows rimmed Tawny-Lynn's big eyes, but Peyton looked much calmer than he expected. Still, when they spotted the group in the office, they both halted warily.

Shouts and chaos erupted.

"Oh, my God!"

"Peyton Boulder?"

"You've been hiding your sister!"

Chaz stepped in front of the two women, a protective stance. "If everyone will calm down, I'll explain."

"You knew she was alive?" Mr. Marx asked.

"Why did you leave our girls to die?" Mrs. Pullman demanded.

Chaz motioned for them to be quiet with his hand. "I've called a press conference in an hour to announce this arrest. Now everyone listen."

A strained hush fell over the room. Chaz stepped aside and ushered Tawny-Lynn and Peyton inside, then separated them from the ill-tempered group by indicating they stand behind the desk.

His father was shooting daggers through both the Boulder girls, his mother wringing her hands together, the others in the room studying them in muted shock.

"Now," Chaz began. "Peyton Boulder survived the crash seven years ago, but she ran and left town out of fear."

"What were you afraid of?" His father asked. "That everyone would find out you were a tramp?"

Chaz spun toward his father. "Dad, if you say one more word, I'm going to throw you in a cell. Now shut up and listen."

Mrs. Wake leaned into her husband's lawyer as if her legs were about to buckle. If she hadn't known about her husband's affairs, he felt sorry for her.

Then again, everyone was innocent until proven guilty. But he believed Peyton's story.

He gestured toward Peyton. "I'm sorry that I ran," Peyton said. "But I was scared."

"Scared of what?" Mrs. Pullman asked gently.

Peyton sank into the chair behind the desk. Tawny-Lynn stood behind her with her hand on Peyton's shoulder for support. Then she spilled her story, the same one she'd told Chaz.

Gasps of outrage and sorrow rumbled through the room. "Did he pressure our daughters into sex?" Mr. Marx asked.

Pain radiated in Peyton's eyes. "I don't know. Honestly. We…never talked about it. In fact, I didn't tell anyone except Ruth. She knew I had a crush on him and, when he approached her, she wanted me to know. I realized then that he was a user and told her to go to her parents. The coach met up with her after the game, and she told him she was going to tell her parents. He exploded and threatened us."

She rubbed her temple, her voice strained. "I saw his car come up behind the bus, then he hit us and the bus spun out of control. I guess I hit my head when we went over the embankment, because when

I came to, blood was everywhere. My sister was on the floor, trapped, and I dragged her out. But I didn't see Ruth anywhere. I was running back to try to save the other girls, but…the bus suddenly burst into flames." Tears trickled down her face, her voice cracking on a sob. "I—I'm so sorry, I wanted to help them, but fire was shooting out on all sides. And I couldn't get back in."

A deafening silence fell across the room, everyone lost in bitter memories and grief and the horrific images Peyton had painted in their heads. Images that obviously tortured Peyton every day.

"What happened then?" Mrs. Pullman asked as she dried her own eyes.

"I saw Coach Wake at the top of the ravine where the bus went over. He was watching the bus burn."

Gasps of outrage filled the room. "That son of a bitch," Mr. Marx muttered.

"I can't believe he just stood there," Mrs. Pullman whispered.

Peyton nodded, the shock of the memory haunting her eyes. "Then I realized that if Coach could just stand there and watch, that he would make good on his threats. That he'd kill me to keep me from going to the sheriff, so I ran."

Mrs. Wake had stood by and listened, but her cheeks blazed with anger. "My husband… He wouldn't have left those girls like that. He was their mentor. He cared about them."

Peyton's gaze rose to meet the woman's. "He did

leave them, Mrs. Wake. I'm sorry, and I don't mean to hurt you. I was a stupid teenager back then, but he slept with me, and then he tried to sleep with Ruth. And he caused the others to die that day."

Mrs. Wake planted her hands on her hips. "No, you seduced him and now you've come back to ruin his reputation."

"That's not true," Peyton said. "I came back to do the right thing because Ruth is dead."

Mrs. Wake moved toward Peyton, but the lawyer caught her. "Come on, this is not helping. We'll talk to your husband and get to the bottom of this."

Chaz faced the group. "Folks, I know you're angry and feel like exacting your own revenge, but you will go home and let me handle this situation the legal way."

Mr. Marx started to protest, but Chaz ushered the parents out the door with a stiff reminder that he'd lock them up if they interfered with the case.

Mrs. Wake had dropped into a chair and was massaging her belly. As soon as the parents left, Lambert and the coach's wife demanded to see Wake. Chaz's parents hovered, as well.

His mother knelt by Peyton and squeezed her hands. "I know you loved Ruth."

"I did," Peyton said in a low voice. "I'm so sorry. I thought— I'd hoped that she'd escaped that day. I didn't know he'd killed her."

His father wasn't as forgiving. "If you'd stuck

around and come to us, maybe we would have found her in time and she'd still be alive."

"That's not fair." Tawny-Lynn stepped in front of Peyton and jutted her chin up at his father. "First you blamed me, now Peyton. My sister tried to warn Ruth about the coach. He's the one you should be mad at, not her."

"Dad," Chaz warned, breaking up the staring contest between Tawny-Lynn and his father. "Take Mother home. I have a press conference in a few minutes."

"You'll let everyone know you caught Ruth's killer?" his father said.

Chaz nodded. "I can't divulge details, but I will announce his arrest and the charges we're filing. But you and Mom remain low key, and don't stir up any more trouble. The last thing I want is for the town to crucify Wake, or for some kind of vigilante to make things worse."

If that happened, he'd have to protect Wake.

And that was the last thing Chaz wanted to do.

He needed to keep him behind bars before his anger got the best of him and he beat the man to a bloody pulp himself.

A SHUDDER COURSED up Tawny-Lynn's spine. She'd known for years that Chaz's father hated her, but his animosity toward Peyton made her furious.

Couldn't he see that Peyton had suffered? She'd left her home out of fear, run because a mentor and man she'd trusted had used her and threatened her. And she'd lost Ruth.

She saw the guilt in her sister's eyes, but she didn't know how to alleviate it. Maybe in time Peyton would be able to forgive herself.

She gave Mr. Camden a cool look, then took Peyton's arm. "Come on, sis, let's go home. A little more work, and we can hang that for-sale sign and both of us can leave this horrible town behind us."

But the memories would haunt them forever.

So would Chaz's handsome face. Why had she gone and fallen in love with him?

His troubled gaze met hers. "You should be safe now, but let me know if there's any more trouble." He angled his head toward Peyton. "Will you write out everything you've told us and sign it? Then I'll let you know when the trial date is set so you can come back and testify."

So that was it? Chaz was resorting back to business as if nothing personal had happened between them.

"Of course," Peyton said.

Tawny-Lynn's heart was breaking as they left the building. She finally had her sister back and the answers she'd yearned for.

But she would never have the man she loved.

Chapter Nineteen

Chaz finished the press conference with a knot in his gut. He wanted to see Tawny-Lynn again, but she probably hated him now. After all, he'd been rough on her when they'd found Ruth.

He would deal with his feelings for her later. Today he had a job to do, and that meant tying up this case so Coach Wake would never see the light of day again.

With the story airing at noon, word would spread quickly in the small town. He'd left his deputy with Wake's lawyer and wife, and was grateful they'd left by the time he made it back to his office.

He had a message to call the M.E. and another from the lab. He phoned the M.E. first. "What did you find?"

"Unfortunately we didn't find any DNA from Coach Wake," the M.E. said. "There were some broken ribs, which probably happened in the accident. We think that she fell backward on a sharp object and hit her head. Could have been a rock. That's what killed her."

Chaz mentally pieced together the facts. Ruth must have crawled out of the bus, and Wake saw her. He chased her, maybe caught up with her and they argued. Then he pushed her and she fell and hit her head.

"Is that all you found?"

"I'm afraid so. Any DNA that might have been under her nails was long ago washed away by the elements and decomp."

"Thanks." He hung up and phoned the crime lab, hoping they had more. "This is Sheriff Camden. Tell me you have good news."

"Nothing condemning yet, but we're trying to recover some DNA from one of the stones left at the gravesite."

"You think it's the one that killed her?"

"No, but the way it was stuck in the ground indicates it might have been used as a grave marker."

Chaz contemplated what he'd said. Had Wake marked the grave so he could come back and visit Ruth? Or maybe he'd planned to move her at some point?

"How about the bracelet?"

"There's a partial print we're working on. I'll let you know if we find a match."

A knock sounded on his door, and the deputy poked his head in. "Sheriff, there's a couple of people here to see you."

Chaz frowned. So the circus was starting.

He thanked the crime tech, then strode into the

front area and was surprised to see Cindy Miller Parker and Rudy Farnsworth standing together.

"We need to talk to you," Cindy said.

Rudy bit down on her lip. "It's important. It's about the coach."

Chaz's stomach knotted. Surely to God they weren't here to say Peyton was lying.

"All right. Can I get you ladies something to drink? Coffee? Water?"

They both shook their heads, half-clinging to each other as he led them into his office. "Okay, what can I do for you?"

Cindy cleared her throat. "We heard about Coach Wake's arrest, and that Peyton Boulder said Coach seduced her."

Chaz nodded, steepling his hands on his desk and waiting.

"What she said is true," Rudy said, her voice quivering.

"How do you know?" Chaz asked.

They spoke at the same time, both looking straight at him with conviction. "Because he did the same thing to us."

"I KNOW THAT was difficult for you," Tawny-Lynn told her sister after they'd eaten lunch.

Peyton shrugged. "It felt good to finally come clean." She gave a sad smile. "I'm so sorry I left you to deal with the fallout after the bus crash."

"I'm sorry you felt like you couldn't come to Dad or me," Tawny-Lynn said.

Peyton shrugged. "Maybe one day we'll stop saying I'm sorry."

Tawny-Lynn lifted her glass of tea in a toast. "Let it be today. It's time to move forward from the past."

Peyton picked up her plate and carried it to the dishwasher. "Right. Now what can I do around here to help you get this place ready to sell?"

"The rain hasn't set in yet, so let's work outside," Tawny-Lynn suggested.

"We should probably hire someone to paint the house," Peyton said.

"Probably," Tawny-Lynn agreed. "But I can't afford that right now."

"I'll pay for it," Peyton said. "I have some money saved."

"All right. But you can take the expenses out of the ranch when we sell it."

"Who knows," Peyton said. "When you fix this place up, you might not want to leave."

Tawny-Lynn's heart squeezed. "I have to. I can't stay here."

"Why not?" Peyton said. "Is there someone special waiting in Austin?"

"No," Tawny-Lynn said. "Just my business."

"Maybe Camden Crossing needs a good landscaper. I saw several new developments going up on my way into town."

Tawny-Lynn shrugged. "It's just too difficult to be here, Peyton."

"Because of what happened, or because of Chaz?"

She narrowed her eyes. "Why would you ask about him?"

"I saw the way you two looked at each other," Peyton said. "You're in love with him, aren't you?"

Tawny-Lynn hadn't been close to anyone in so long that it felt strange to have her sister back watching her, reading her so well. "He doesn't feel the same way," she said instead of denying the truth.

"Are you sure about that?" Peyton asked. "Because it looked to me like he was crazy about you."

"His family hates me," she said. "Mr. Camden crucified me after the crash, accused me of intentionally holding back information about you and Ruth."

"I'm sure he didn't mean it."

"Oh, he meant it all right. You know Chaz's father is rich and owns the town. He turned others against me. I would never be good enough for his son."

Peyton caught her arm. "If Chaz loves you, it doesn't matter what his father thinks."

"That's just it," she said, her voice cracking. "He doesn't love me." She headed to the kitchen sink. "Now, enough about the Camdens. I thought we'd plant some rosebushes today."

Peyton teared up again. "Let's plant yellow roses in the place where Ruth was buried."

Tawny-Lynn stacked her own plate in the dishwasher. Yellow roses for friendship seemed appropriate.

Tawny-Lynn's cell phone buzzed. She glanced at the caller ID and saw it was Chaz, so she snatched it up. "Hello."

"I wanted to let you and Peyton know that Cindy Miller Parker and Rudy Farnsworth came in my office after the press conference."

She frowned. "Really? Were they shocked about the coach?"

Chaz made a low sound of disgust. "No. In fact, they both made statements that Coach Wake pressured them into having sex when they were in school, too."

Tawny-Lynn paused. No wonder they'd been standoffish when she'd approached them. "So they'll testify and back up Peyton's story?"

"Yes, so tell Peyton she's not alone in this."

Thank God.

"I have to go. I'm going to push Wake for a confession now, so we can speed this process along."

Tawny-Lynn ended the call, then turned and told Peyton.

"I'm sorry he did the same thing to them," Peyton said.

"Me, too," Tawny-Lynn murmured. "But with their testimonies, the charges should stick."

Peyton nodded, that haunted look back. "Let's go plant those roses for Ruth."

FOR HOURS, CHAZ fended off calls from local citizens asking about Coach Wake's arrest. Parents were freaking out, wanting to know details—if he'd only targeted girls or if he'd sexually abused boys. When? How many?

The questions went on and on.

He finally let the machine pick up, deciding he'd listen to the messages. If anyone had pertinent information, he'd return the call.

A knock sounded on his office door, and his deputy poked his head in. "Sheriff, there's a couple of people here who insist on seeing you."

Chaz stood. "All right. Check the messages and let me know if we need to follow up on any of them."

When he stepped into the front, two sets of parents were waiting, along with two teenage girls.

"I'm Sheriff Camden," Chaz said. "What can I do for you?"

One of the fathers spoke up. "My name is Joe Lansing. We want to press charges against Coach Wake."

Chaz glanced back and forth between them. "Go on."

The mother of the first girl wrapped her arm around her daughter, a petite blonde they introduced as Joan. "After we saw the news, Joan came o me. She told me the coach forced her to have sex with him this past year."

Chaz narrowed his eyes at the girl. "Is that true?"

Joan lowered her head and nodded. "I was afraid o tell anyone. He said he'd cut me from the team."

"He said he loved me," the other girl said. "That f I wanted to play first string, I'd show him I loved him, too."

Chaz hesitated. He'd read about cases where eenagers made up stories to get attention. But the nore he talked to the girls, the more he was convinced they were telling the truth.

"I'll need your statements written down," he said. 'And will you testify in court?"

They both agreed, and so did the parents. Then he watched as the girls wrote out details that sickened him and made him want to go after Coach Wake all over again.

By the time they'd left, his deputy joined him with three more complaints from girls whose parents had called in. He phoned them all back and explained they would need to make formal statements.

Apparently, after word leaked about the coach's arrest, the team had met and the parents had encouraged their daughters to break the code of silence, that confessing what the coach had done didn't reflect badly upon them.

He admired them for their courage.

He strode back to the jail cell with the other two complaints in his hand.

Coach Wake stood, his anger palpable. "When is my arraignment? I want out of this hellhole."

Chaz folded his arms. "I don't think that's going to happen, Coach. I have two more written statements here from girls you've coached confirming that you forced them to have sex with you. And I'm getting calls about more."

"They're lying," Coach Wake said, although fear laced his voice.

"Really? You mean Peyton Boulder came all the way back here after seven years of silence to lie. So did Cindy Miller and Rudy Farnsworth. And those girls on your current team are lying, too."

"They wanted to have sex," he shouted bitterly. "They asked for it!"

"My sister didn't ask for it," Chaz said between clenched teeth. "In fact, she was going to tell my parents."

"She just wanted to play hard to get," Coach Wake muttered.

Chaz fisted his hands. He wanted to wrap them around the sicko's neck. "No, Ruth wasn't like that. You used your power and influence to rope the girls into your bed. And Peyton had the courage to stand up to you. Others have found it, too."

Chaz swallowed back bile. "In fact, Ruth stood up against you. That's why you killed her."

"I didn't kill her." Coach Wake's voice cracked. "I admit I had sex with Peyton and the other girls, and I was mad and chased after the bus, but I didn't mean to run into it. My car hit a wet patch and I skidded. It was an accident."

"An accident, but you stood and watched the bus explode and didn't even try to help those girls inside."

"It happened too fast. There was nothing I could do."

Chaz wasn't buying it—Wake was a lowdown coward. "You were angry and afraid your dirty secret would come out, so you found Ruth and killed her, then buried her out at White Forks to make the police think Peyton's father killed her."

Coach Wake gripped the bars. "I didn't kill Ruth. I saw Peyton pull Tawny-Lynn from the bus, then he went back, and I figured she'd get Ruth out. Then I heard a car coming."

"So instead of going down to try and rescue the other girls, you ran off and left them there in that burning bus."

Resignation and sorrow, the man's first hint at true emotions, lined the coach's face as he sank onto the cot again. "I panicked—I just panicked—and then I was scared to come forward. I didn't want to go to jail."

"So you let those girls die, then stood by while the town crucified Tawny-Lynn. Then you went back to your same old ways, sexually assaulting the students who trusted you."

"You don't understand, the girls, they're so young and flirty—"

"They are minors, teenagers, students who trusted you, and you took advantage of them."

Coach Wake scraped a hand over his chin. "So had sex with some of them, but I didn't kill Ruth," Coach Wake said firmly. "I swear I didn't."

Chaz studied the man with a sick feeling in his belly. Wake had just admitted to sexual assault and causing the accident. So if he'd killed Ruth, why not confess to that, too?

Unless he hadn't murdered her...

But if he hadn't, who had?

Wake's wife's face flashed in his mind. She'd defended her husband. What if she'd known he was cheating with those younger girls?

She could have followed the bus or even been following her husband, then killed Ruth.

TAWNY-LYNN COLLAPSED into bed exhausted from the day's ordeal and the manual work she and Peyton had done outside. Not only had they planted flowers, but they'd cleaned out the barn, bought pine straw and spread wood chips around several trees in the yard nearest the house.

Knowing Coach Wake was in jail and Peyton was sleeping in the next room, she fell into a deep sleep. Surely the nightmares would leave her in peace now.

But some time later, a cold chill stirred her from sleep. The room was dark, the scent of a man's

ologne suffusing her. She gasped, the dark blank
ace that had haunted her for years was back.

She blinked, hoping she was dreaming, but when
he opened her eyes, he was there. Coming toward
er.

She tried to scream, but a hand clamped over
er mouth, then she felt the cold barrel of a gun
gainst her temple.

Chapter Twenty

Chaz stewed over his conversation with the coach long into the night when he should have been sleeping.

Wake would go down for multiple counts of manslaughter for the bus driver and three teens. Coupled with the sexual assault charges, he would spend years in prison.

So why not confess to Ruth's murder?

His phone trilled, making the nerves in his neck tighten. Yesterday he'd thought he'd solved the cold case and maybe the town could heal. But now he wasn't so sure.

Another peal of the phone and he saw the number for White Forks on the caller ID screen. He gripped the phone, knowing it could be Peyton or Tawny-Lynn. "Sheriff Camden."

"Chaz, it's Peyton. Someone took Tawny-Lynn."

"What?" Cold sweat burst on his brow.

"I heard a scream and ran to her room, but she wasn't inside," Peyton cried. "Then I ran down the steps and saw someone in dark clothes dragging her outside."

"Who was it?"

"I don't know, I couldn't see. I'm scared, Chaz." A sob from Peyton echoed over the line. "You have to find her."

His mind raced. Tawny-Lynn had been in danger since she'd pulled into town. After making the arrest, he assumed Coach Wake had been trying to scare her into leaving and keeping quiet.

But now?

"Chaz, I can't lose her," Peyton said. "Not when just got her back."

He couldn't lose her, either. Not that she'd ever been his. But they had made love. And he'd thought she cared about him.

Then he'd blown it by hurling accusations at her.

"Tell me what else you saw. Was it a man or a woman?"

"I don't know," Peyton said. "It was so dark outside and whoever it was had on black clothes and a hood."

"Did her abductor say anything?"

"No, but I thought I saw something shiny glint in the darkness. I...think it was a gun."

His stomach knotted. "Lock the doors, Peyton. I'm going to send my deputy out there while I look for your sister."

Peyton agreed in a shaky voice, and he ended the call, then phoned his deputy and explained. "I don't want Peyton left alone for a minute. She may be in danger."

"I'm on my way," Deputy Lemone said.

Chaz hung up, grabbed his gun and holster and strapped it on. Several people in town, especially the parents of the girls in the crash, along with his own parents, had despised Tawny-Lynn for years. But after the arrest, there was no reason to go after her.

The only person he could think of with motive was the coach's wife. She was pregnant and obviously distraught over the accusations against her husband. She wouldn't want the father of her baby in prison when her child was born.

And maybe she thought that Tawny-Lynn had seen him—or her—at the crash site that day with Ruth.

He raced to his car and sped toward the Wake's house, praying that she hadn't hurt Tawny-Lynn.

TAWNY-LYNN STIRRED from unconsciousness. As soon as her abductor had gotten her to the car, he'd knocked her over the back of her head with the butt of his gun.

She blinked through the darkness, trying to see him and figure out where they were.

"Good, you're awake. Now it's time to write your suicide note."

Fear seized her at the sound of the voice. A very familiar voice.

She blinked again, struggling to sit up, then realized her legs and wrists were bound. He gripped her arm and hauled her to a sitting position.

Moonlight illuminated the dark face. The one that had been blank all these years.

Now it slid into focus.

Chaz's father.

Suddenly the past rushed back to her. She had roused from unconsciousness that day. And she'd seen him dragging Ruth away. Ruth was crying and shouting for him to let her go, but then Mr. Camden had struck her. Ruth fell against a rock, then the world had gone dark for her again.

"Why are you doing this?" she asked, her heart hammering. "Chaz arrested the coach. And I didn't remember anything."

"But you would have," he growled. "It was only a matter of time. I saw the way you looked at me yesterday." He shoved a notepad and pen into her hands. "You seduced my son, too. I can't take the chance—"

"On Chaz learning that you killed Ruth," Tawny-Lynn spat out. "You were at the crash site that day. You grabbed her and were arguing—"

Pain wrenched his face. "It was an accident," he said, his voice warbling. "She told me about Coach Wake and wanted me to go public."

"But you didn't want her to, did you?" Tawny Lynn started struggling with her hands, but he pressed the gun to her chest and she froze.

"Of course not," he snapped. "Everyone would have talked about it, talked about her, thought she was a slut. I couldn't let that happen."

"You could have stood up for her and stopped the coach," Tawny-Lynn said. "Instead you cared more about your pride and appearances, and your daughter died for it."

He gripped her arms and shook her. "Shut up. I told you it was an accident."

"Then why did you hide it? And how could you put her in the ground instead of giving her a proper burial?"

Tears streamed down his face. "I wanted to bury her right," he said. "But my wife wouldn't have understood. And Chaz… He would have hated me."

"So you turned the town against me?"

"Because if your sister hadn't started the affair with Coach Wake, he never would have come after Ruth."

"You're delusional," Tawny-Lynn said. "Chaz called me last night and said two other girls from our class came forward and made the same accusations. Who knows how many more girls will speak up now?"

"It doesn't matter," Camden said. "My wife and Chaz can't find out what happened that day, they

:an't." He tapped the notepad. "Now take that pen and write what I tell you to."

"Please, you don't have to do this," Tawny-Lynn whispered.

He jammed the pen between her fingers.

"No one will ever believe I killed myself," Tawny-Lynn said.

"Oh, yes, they will," Camden said in a sinister voice. "You're going to confess that you were jealous of Ruth and your sister, jealous of Ruth and the coach, and that you pushed Ruth down and made her fall."

CHAZ WAS SURPRISED to see a light on in Mrs. Wake's house. He glanced through the front living room window, searching for movement.

Footsteps sounded inside, and he held his gun at the ready in case Mrs. Wake was armed. How else would she have been able to force Tawny-Lynn from the ranch house?

He didn't see anything through the front window so he moved to the side and peered in. The window gave him a view of the kitchen where he saw Mrs. Wake pacing with her hand over her belly. She doubled over and cried out, and Chaz froze.

Was she in labor?

He eased around the side of the house, looking in other windows, but it was dark and he couldn't see anything. He craned his head to listen for sounds indicating Tawny-Lynn was inside, but nothing.

Finally he moved back to the kitchen window and saw Mrs. Wake collapse into a chair, one hand reaching for her phone. She knocked it off the table and leaned her head on her hands, heaving as she breathed through the contraction.

Dammit. Did she have Tawny-Lynn?

He circled back to the front door and pounded on it. Afraid the woman was in trouble, he jiggled the door but it was locked. "Mrs. Wake, it's Sheriff Camden. Open up please."

Seconds bled into minutes, then he heard her feet shuffling. When she opened the door, her face was contorted in pain, and she was clutching her belly.

"You're in labor?"

"How did you know?" she asked through a deep breath.

"I didn't. I'm looking for Tawny-Lynn Boulder."

Her cheeks reddened with exertion as she gripped the door. "Why would I know where she is?"

"Because someone kidnapped her from her house tonight."

Her eyes widened in shock, but another contraction seized her, and her legs buckled. He caught her before she hit the floor and put his arm around her waist.

"Come on, I'll drive you to the hospital."

"I need my husband," she whispered.

That wasn't going to happen. "Is Tawny-Lynn here?" he asked.

She shook her head. "Of course not." She made

panting sounds as he helped her to the car. She fell into the seat, her face ashen.

He had to get her to the E.R. But he had to search the house first just in case she was lying.

"I'll be right back."

"Where are you going?" she cried.

He didn't answer. He ran back in the house, racing through each room and flipping on lights. He searched closets, the pantry, the attic, but the house was empty.

He noticed a suitcase on the floor and assumed it was Mrs. Wake's so he grabbed it and jogged down the steps. She was clutching the seat, heaving through another contraction, when he jumped inside.

"I got your bag."

"Get me to the hospital," she said. "Or I'm going to deliver this baby in your car."

He flipped on the siren and peeled from the drive. Thankfully traffic was nonexistent and the hospital was close by. Five minutes later, he roared into the emergency room driveway and threw the car into Park. He jumped out, yelling for help.

"This woman is about to deliver," he said as two E.R. workers raced out to meet him.

"Please, Sheriff, my husband should be here."

"I'm sorry." He couldn't make that happen right now, not with Tawny-Lynn missing and in danger. And his deputy was guarding Peyton. "Is there anyone else I can call?"

She shook her head. "My mother." She recited the number, and he called as he jumped back in his car. Five rings later, a woman answered, her voice laced with sleep.

"This is Sheriff Camden. Your daughter asked me to call you. She's in labor. I just dropped her at the hospital."

"Oh, thank you, Sheriff. I'll get there as soon as I can."

His phone was buzzing with another call as he pulled away. He checked the number and saw it was his mother. Why would she be calling him at 4:00 a.m.?

"Mom?"

"Chaz, I need you," she said in a shaky voice.

"What's wrong?"

"Your father…"

Had his father gone after the coach? "What happened?"

"He's gone."

"Gone where?"

"I don't know, but you have to come over here. We need to talk."

Fear rolled through Chaz. First Tawny-Lynn was kidnapped. Now his father was missing?

What the hell was going on?

He sped away from the hospital, siren blaring as he raced toward his parents' house. Worry clawed at him as he tried to make sense out of the situation. If Wake hadn't killed Ruth, then Tawny-Lynn had een the killer that day after the crash, and the killer was afraid she'd still remember his or her face.

But why do something to his father?

He rounded the curve on two wheels, tires squealing as he swerved up the drive to his parents' estate. Sweat beaded on his head as he threw the car into Park and ran inside.

His mother met him at the door, her complexion pasty, her eyes red-rimmed. She'd been crying. "Oh, Chaz, I'm so afraid."

He hugged her and ushered her into the den to sit down. "What happened, Mom?"

She burst into tears. "I...don't know. He was so upset last night when we got home, and he started drinking. Then he pulled out all the old pictures of Ruth, and then I saw him looking at pictures of the crash and all the articles that ran afterward. The pleas we made for information on Ruth and Peyton, the story about Tawny-Lynn and the story about the coach's arrest."

He handed her a handkerchief and waited while she dried her eyes.

"I tried to talk to him, but he was so upset. Shouting and saying crazy things about blame and guilt and Tawny-Lynn seeing something."

A bad feeling gnawed at his gut. "Then what?"

"He grabbed his gun from his desk and said he had to finish things, to finally put everything to rest."

"What did he mean by that?"

"I don't know," his mother said in a shaky voice "He just said he had to do it for our family. Then he took the gun and left."

"Was he going after Coach Wake?"

"No, I don't think so."

Chaz inhaled sharply. "Mom, Coach Wake admitted that he had sex with the girls and caused the bus crash, but he denied killing Ruth. If you know something, anything...please tell me."

Another storm of tears rained down her face, and she hugged her arms around her middle as if she might fall apart if she let go. "I don't know... not anything really."

Emotions threatened to overwhelm him. "But you suspect something?"

She nodded miserably. "That night...of the accident..." She heaved a sob. "That night I found Ruth's softball bag...I saw him hiding it."

"Dad had her bag?" The bag that was never recovered from the accident. They'd assumed it had burned in the fire.

"Yes. When I asked him, he went crazy and refused to talk about it. I...forgot about it for a while, but tonight when I saw him with the pictures, he had that bag again."

Chaz's blood ran cold. If his father had Ruth's gym bag, that meant he had been at the crash site.

He could have seen Ruth, talked to her...and if she'd told him about the coach...

No...it was impossible.

His father had a temper, had been overprotective of Ruth, had worried about appearances...

Cop instincts kicked in, and his mind took another dangerous leap. His father had been the one to lead the animosity against Tawny-Lynn. He'd barged into her room at the hospital.

Dear God. Had his father killed Ruth?

"You won't get away with this," Tawny-Lynn said as she finished the suicide note. "Chaz will figure out the truth."

Mr. Camden laughed harshly. "No, he won't. If he really does care about you, he'll be devastated to learn that you're the one who killed his sister, and that you used him all this time."

"He's smarter than you think," she said. "He doesn't let emotions interfere with his job." Sadly, she knew that firsthand.

He waved the gun in her face. "Shut up and get out."

"Chaz will never believe I killed myself."

"I'll take care of that." He dragged her toward the ravine. He'd parked at almost exactly the same spot where the bus had gone over the edge seven years ago. It fit with his plan.

Everyone would think that she was overcome with guilt and decided to end her life where she'd taken Ruth's.

"Even if Chaz believes you, my sister won't. Besides, you've forgotten that I had a broken leg.

There's no way I could have killed Ruth." She struggled against him. "How did you get her on White Forks without my father seeing you?"

Mr. Camden's voice trembled. "I buried her while he was at the hospital with you. Now it's time to end this."

He squeezed her arm. "You grabbed Ruth's leg and pushed her down," he said with a shrug of his shoulders. "She hit her head on a rock."

Tawny-Lynn shook her head. "Killing her was an accident. If you explained that Ruth fell, everyone would understand," she said, "but killing me is premeditated murder."

He shoved her toward the edge. "With you gone and your heartfelt confession, no one will ever know about either."

She stumbled forward, the ravine below resurrecting memories of the crash that day. She could hear the screams of the other girls as the bus went over.

Remembered the cries of the parents as they'd arrived. Her terror in searching for Peyton.

She'd finally found Peyton again. She couldn't die like this.

And she couldn't leave this world with Chaz thinking that she'd killed his sister.

Chapter Twenty-One

Panic crowded Chaz's chest. "Mother, someone broke in and abducted Tawny-Lynn tonight. Do you think Dad would hurt her?"

"I don't know, Chaz," she cried. "I've never seen him like this. He was...out of his head."

"I have to find him before he does something to her," he said. "Do you have any idea where he might take her?"

She shook her head as more tears filled her eyes and spilled over. "He just kept saying that the day of the crash ruined our lives. That Tawny-Lynn did."

If he was thinking about the crash, then he might go there, take Tawny-Lynn back to the place where everything had fallen apart.

He squeezed his mother's hands. "I have to go. If you hear from him, call me."

She nodded, terror streaking her face. "Please find him, stop him," she whispered. "If he hurt Ruth, he didn't mean to. But if he hurts Tawny-Lynn—"

"I know," he said. "I know."

He pushed to his feet and jogged back outside. His tires screamed as he accelerated, sped down the drive and veered onto the highway.

He phoned his deputy, relieved when he answered. "How's Peyton?"

"Worried." He paused. "Did you find Tawny-Lynn?"

"Not yet. But I have a lead. Stay with Peyton. I'll call you back."

He hung up, then swung onto the road leading to the bus crash site, his heart throbbing. Dawn was on the horizon, red and orange swirls painting the sky, promising a clear day instead of the rain the weatherman had predicted.

As he rounded the curve, he spotted his father's car on the side of the road, parked sideways, nose heading toward the ravine. He slowed, his breath stalling.

His father stood behind Tawny-Lynn, a gun pressed to her back.

He rolled the car to a stop several hundred feet back, then eased his door open. In spite of the fact that he was careful, gravel crunched beneath his boots as he slowly walked toward them.

His father swung his head toward him. His mother was right. He'd never seen his father looking so crazed. He tightened his hold on Tawny-Lynn's arm. "Don't come any closer, Chaz."

"Dad, you have to stop this right now," Chaz said. "You don't want to hurt Tawny-Lynn."

"She has to die—don't you see that?" his father snarled. "She saw me that day. She'll ruin everything for our family."

"It's not her fault." Chaz's gaze met Tawny-Lynn's. She looked scared, but gave him such a look of sorrow and trust that he nearly choked on his love for her.

Love?

Yes, he did love her, he realized. But he'd been such a fool that he'd never told her.

Instead he'd run from his feelings for her by turning on her like everyone in the town had.

TAWNY-LYNN HATED the anguish in Chaz's eyes. She'd never once suspected his father of killing Ruth. And neither had Chaz.

He had to be in shock.

"Just walk away, Chaz, and let me handle this. You'll see. She wrote out a confession." He waved the barrel of the gun at her temple. "She was jealous of Ruth and Peyton, jealous of the coach because he wanted Ruth, not her. Isn't that right, Tawny-Lynn?"

She cut him a scathing look. "You know that's not what happened, Mr. Camden."

"I can't lose my family," Camden said, anger radiating from his every pore. "I won't."

"You will if you kill Tawny-Lynn, Dad," Chaz said in a gruff voice. "Right now, Mom and I know that what happened with Ruth was an accident. But doing this, intentionally hurting Tawny-Lynn is no the same thing."

"I didn't mean to do it," he said. "Ruth was arguing with me. She said she was going to tell everyone about Coach Wake. I just tried to stop her and I grabbed her arm, but she fell. Her head hit a rock." Tears clogged his voice. "I loved Ruth...."

"I know that, and so does Mom." Chaz slowly inched toward his father.

"We can forgive that, Dad. It was an accident. But we can't forgive you if you hurt Tawny-Lynn."

His father's hand trembled, the gun shaking as he waved it back and forth between himself and Tawny-Lynn.

"Dad, please put down the gun." Chaz held out his hand. "Just set it on the ground and we'll talk."

"No, then everyone will know..." He swung the gun up and aimed it at his own head, and fear seized Tawny-Lynn. If Chaz's father killed himself, Chaz would never get over the guilt.

Camden clenched his hand tighter on the gun, but Tawny-Lynn threw a sharp jab to his side with her elbow and knocked his gun hand up into the air. The gun fired, a bullet flying upward, but in his panic, Camden shoved her aside.

Chaz lunged toward his father, wrestling for the gun. The gun fired again, but Chaz managed to wrangle it from his father's hands and tossed it a few yards away, then threw his father onto the ground.

She stumbled, lost her footing and slid. Gravel ained down the ravine as she slipped over the side.

She screamed, grappling for something to hold on to so she wouldn't plunge into the ravine below.

CHAZ FRANTICALLY SEIZED his father's hands and yanked them behind his back, then snapped handcuffs around his wrists. He didn't want to arrest him, but he had to take him in.

Tawny-Lynn's scream brought him out of his shock, and he jerked his head up and saw her going over the edge. She'd saved his father's life by throwing that punch.

He couldn't let her die.

"Stay put, Dad," Chaz said in a low growl in his father's ear. He ran to the edge of the embankment, then knelt. Tawny-Lynn had managed to grab a rock jutting out, but dirt and gravel were spewing down the embankment in her face, and her fingers were slipping.

"Hang on," he shouted. "I've got you."

He wrapped his fingers around one wrist, then reached for the other hand but she lost hold. Her hand missed, and she dangled over the ravine. His arm muscles strained as he braced himself in the dirt and stretched to reach for her.

"Chaz!" she cried. "I can't hold on."

"Yes, you can! You have to," he said. "Trust me."

She was trembling, her body flailing to grab hold. He fell to his belly and stretched, finally latching on to her other arm. Her fingers dug into his wrist, and he grunted and slowly hauled her up over the edge, crawling backward and pulling her with him until they were safely away from the overhang.

His father lifted his head and looked up, his expression defeated as Chaz folded Tawny-Lynn into his arms.

"I'm sorry," he whispered into her hair.

"I...didn't remember, not until tonight."

No wonder she'd blocked it out. "I know, I know." He cupped her face between his hands and checked her for injuries. "Are you all right?"

She nodded, although tears trickled down her face. "I'm sorry, Chaz.... Sorry about Ruth."

"Shh," he murmured. Then he wrapped her in his embrace. "I love you, Tawny-Lynn. I was so afraid I was going to lose you before I could tell you."

She looked into his eyes, the sweet passionate, courageous woman he'd come to know staring back. "I love you, too, Chaz."

His heart swelled with emotions, with the need to hold her, possess her, to keep her near.

They had to talk about the future, deal with his father, with his mother...

But not yet.

For now, he bent his head and kissed her, savoring the fact that she was alive and in his arms.

Epilogue

Tawny-Lynn couldn't believe how happy she was. Today was her wedding day.

Peyton peeked in, then straightened her veil. "You look beautiful, sis."

"Thanks." Tawny-Lynn hugged her sister, thanking God every day that Peyton had survived. "I like Ben."

Peyton smiled. "He's a good guy. He's been patient with me. And—" she wiggled her finger, a diamond glittering on her left hand "—he asked me to marry him."

"That's wonderful." They hugged through their tears, then Peyton pulled away, grabbed them tissues and laughed. "Now, stop crying or you'll mess up your makeup."

Tawny-Lynn dried her eyes, and Peyton hurried to the door. "Come on, they're about to play the wedding march!"

A sliver of sadness dampened her mood as she opened the door and saw Chaz's mother sitting

alone in the front row in one of the chairs they'<
set up for the ceremony. Arresting Chaz's fathe<
had torn Chaz apart, but he didn't blame Tawny
Lynn. He'd had to do it for Ruth.

His father had pleaded guilty to kidnapping an<
threatening her, and was spending time in a psych<
atric facility to receive counseling. Mrs. Camden
though heartbroken about her husband, had actu<
ally apologized to Tawny-Lynn for the brutal wa<
they'd treated her years ago. Occasionally thing<
were tense, but they were working hard at a rela
tionship because they both loved Chaz.

She and Peyton had decided to keep the ranch
Chaz was moving in with her and planned to hel<
her repair the house. Cindy Miller had introduce<
Tawny-Lynn to her husband who'd hired her to d<
all the landscaping at the new developments aroun<
town.

For a girl who'd felt shunned by the town, she
finally felt a part of it.

Peyton had worked with one of their old classmates, Andrea Radcliff, who had opened a brida
shop, to set up the wedding on the lawn of the
ranch. With the garden she'd planted, a gazebc
draped in lace and fresh flowers and a white tent
complete with champagne and wedding cake, the
place looked gorgeous and more romantic than she
could have imagined.

Peyton, dressed in a summery pale blue sun-ress, carried a bouquet of lilies. Tawny-Lynn miled as she followed her sister down the center isle between the rows of white chairs.

When she saw Chaz standing at the foot of the azebo in his long, dark duster and cowboy hat, her eart leaped with joy.

CHAZ'S GAZE MET his bride-to-be's beautiful eyes, nd he couldn't believe this day had finally arrived.

The day he was going to make Tawny-Lynn his vife.

His deputy surprised him by admitting that he played guitar, and now was strumming the wedding march as Tawny-Lynn walked down the aisle.

She was so beautiful that it made his heart hurt every time he thought about the fact that he'd almost lost her. That wild wheat-colored hair of hers fluttered in the wind as she approached, the red oses she carried stark against the soft, white, strapess dress hugging her curves.

He couldn't wait to take it off her.

She paused in front of him, and he took her hand nd led her up the steps of the gazebo. The reverend commenced the short ceremony, and minutes ater, announced them man and wife.

Chaz turned to Tawny-Lynn and framed her face etween his hands. "I love you, Mrs. Camden."

"I love you, too," she whispered.

Then he claimed her mouth with his lips, pouring his heart and love into their first kiss as husband and wife.

* * * * *

Look for the sequel to
COLD CASE AT CAMDEN CROSSING,
COLD CASE AT CARLTON'S CANYON,
featuring Texas Ranger Justin Thorpe and
Sheriff Amanda Blair as they tackle
the case of the missing girls from Sunset Mesa

Coming January 2014,
only from Harlequin Intrigue!

ReaderService.com

Manage your account online!

- Review your order history
- Manage your payments
- Update your address

Enjoy all the features!

- Reader excerpts from any series
- Respond to mailings and special monthly offers
- Discover new series available to you
- Browse the Bonus Bucks catalog
- Share your feedback

Visit us at:
ReaderService.com

RS13

LARGER-PRINT BOOKS!

GET 2 FREE LARGER-PRINT NOVELS PLUS 2 FREE MYSTERY GIFTS

Love Inspired

SUSPENSE
RIVETING INSPIRATIONAL ROMANCE

Larger-print novels are now available...